The Wounded Nurse | Alex Amit

Printed in the United States of America

First Printing, 2022
Line Editing: Grace Michaeli

Contact: alex@authoralexamit.com
http://authoralexamit.com/

ISBN: 9798843855680

The Wounded Nurse

Part 2

Alex Amit

11. One of us.

The hospital's front driveway is quiet in the fall afternoon as I sit on the stairs, gasping and catching my breath after walking on the main road. I must keep practicing so no one will notice my limping.

I carefully lift my khaki pants and scratch my sore legs, cautious not to bruise the sensitive skin. For a moment I think of loosening the prosthetic leg's leather straps and rubbing the stump. But when I raise my gaze, I hear an army jeep approaching from the main road, swiftly entering the hospital's front driveway, and I pull down my khaki pants and watch as it stops near me.

"Good afternoon." Two officers are sitting in the green and noisy jeep, and one of them is talking to me. They are both wearing leather aviation jackets, visors, and sunglasses, as if they've just come out of a pilot recruitment ad, like the ones I used to see back home.

"Good afternoon," I reply, gently stroking my sore leg through my pants and lowering my gaze, feeling my sweat.

"Can you please call Audrey and her friend, and tell them we've arrived?"

"They'll be out soon." I keep on sitting on the stairs. If I start walking, they'll see my limp.

"Then we'll wait for them," he answers and smiles as he gets out of the jeep. He leans against the hood, placing his hand on the white American star painted on the jeep's green and khaki camouflage.

Should I say anything to them? Be nice to them? I look at the cypress trees on either side of the entrance to the mansion, searching for something to focus on, anything but them.

"Nice to meet you, I'm Henry." He holds out his hand after a while.

"Grace. Nice to meet you." I look and smile at him, reaching my hand out without getting up. He approaches me and we shake hands, not before he takes off his sunglasses for a moment. He has a tanned face and short brown hair, several medals and decorations are pinned to his chest, and he is smiling at me.

"Are you new here?" he asks.

"Yes." I don't want to tell him about my past here. Why are Audrey and her friend not coming out already?

"We're from the airfield beyond the hill."

"I've heard about you."

"Are you one of the female truck drivers here?" He continues the polite conversation, pointing to my khaki uniform and the army trucks parked on the side.

"Are you one of the bomber drivers?"

"Yes, I think so," he laughs, still holding the sunglasses in his hand. "I've never thought of myself as a bomber driver."

"What plane do you drive?"

"A B-17 bomber. What truck do you drive?"

For a moment I wanted to tell him I'm driving a wooden leg, but I was ashamed.

"I'm not really a driver," I look down.

"And I'm not really a pilot," he replies, despite the leather jacket and pilot wings attached to it. His friend, who got out of the jeep, smiles.

"You're obviously a pilot, you have pilots' sunglasses."

"Here, take them," he hands them to me. "I'm just using them to show off."

"And what will I do with them?"

"You could say you're an army truck pilot."

"I'm a nurse," I finally reply, looking into his eyes. He has brown eyes. Why are they not coming out?

"Sorry, my mistake, I apologize," he smiles at me. "I didn't think you were a nurse because of the khaki uniform."

"Yes, she likes to be different," I hear Audrey laugh as she and another nurse come down the hospital stairs. She walks over to greet Henry, rising to kiss him on his cheek. "Have you been waiting for us long?"

"I'm always willing to wait for a beautiful woman," he laughs as she takes his hand, pulling him after her and into the jeep waiting for them.

"Have a nice flight," I whisper to them, watching the other nurse hugging her pilot too.

"Being different is good," I hear Henry before he climbs into the jeep, smiling at me.

"Being different is great," I reply. If he only knew how much I hate being different.

"Your glasses," I shout to him, trying to overcome the jeep's noise.

"It's okay. Give them back to me the next time we meet. In the meantime, you can drive your truck."

"Drive what? She's just an intern nurse," I can hear Audrey as the jeep starts moving.

"It was nice to meet you, Grace," he

yells towards me as the jeep moves away. "Come visit us at our club," I can still hear him say, but his voice is already mixed with the sound of the girls' laughter.

"I promise," I quietly say to him and look at the sunglasses in my hand, knowing I'll never have the courage to visit them.

"Come on, Pinocchio's leg, let's go to the room," I whisper to myself after the jeep disappears behind the trees, and I slowly get up and limp to my room. I have a long way to go before I'm accepted to the Pilots' Club.

***

The following days, I'd avoid sitting and resting on the hospitals' front stairs when returning from my walks on the main road. I don't want to see how Audrey hurries to get into that pilot's jeep again, determined to remind me of my place. I also avoid visiting him; he has Edward, who reads to him from the book without destroying the pages with dog-ears, and I have a job as a nurse in an operating room. But I have something for him in my uniform pocket, and I'm careful not to break it. I must go see him.

"Grace, we're done for today, it's actually tomorrow already," the surgeon takes a few steps back from the wounded soldier lying on the operating table, removing the white mask covering his mouth. "Go rest. It's already midnight. You're working too hard." I finish bandaging the wounded soldier, who is sleeping in a cloud of morphine, and then leave the operating room, washing my hands and wiping the sweat off my face.

At the bottom of the stairs, before going up to my room, I stop for a moment and look at the hall of wounded men, trying to get used to the darkness. He must be sleeping by now, I don't see candlelight from where his bed is, nor can I hear Edward reading my book to him. The next time we meet, I can say it was night when I visited him, and he was asleep.

"Gracie, is that you? With the funny steps?" he whispers to me in the dark as I approach him, and although I hate that he can recognize me, I smile.

"How are you?" I touch his fingers.

"I'm sorry I haven't visited for a long time."

"Did you come to read to me? You're lovely, but there's no need. Edward reads to me every morning." John doesn't move the fingers I'm touching.

"I didn't come to read to you. I just passed by." He doesn't need me and doesn't miss our conversations.

"And how are you? Did you fix a lot of wounded soldiers?"

"I brought you something." I sit down on the edge of his bed. I must let my leg rest a little. I'll give him what I brought and go to my room, it's late.

"What did you bring me? Isn't it the middle of the night?"

"Come closer to me."

He sits up in bed, and I light a candle and gently remove the bandage covering his eyes. They've been there for too long by now, and the nurses only keep them there now to hide his injured eyes. My fingers touch and feel the scars on his closed eyelids, and his fingers join mine as he gently caresses his eyes and my fingers.

"It's a strange feeling," he whispers and keeps stroking his eyes, keeps touching my fingers as well.

"You've recovered well." I take what I brought him from my uniform pocket, carefully placing it over his eyes.

"What's this?" He touches the thin frame. "Glasses?"

"Yes, glasses."

"Blind-people glasses?"

"No, pilots' sunglasses." I set them over his eyes.

"Is this the German pilot's glasses?" he asks, and I tense up and cringe. What does he know about the German and me?

"What did you hear about him?"

"Was it you who took care of the German?"

"Where did you hear about that?" I get up from his bed. It's time for me to go.

"Everyone was talking about the nurse no one likes, the one who walks funny," he quietly says. "They say she likes them, the Germans, that she's the only one willing to take care of him, unlike all the other patriotic nurses who refuse to cooperate with the enemy."

What should I tell him? What does it matter anyway? He knows who this limping nurse is. How many limping nurses are there in the world?

"Yes, it's me," I say to him after a while, getting ready to go to sleep in my room. I've had a long day.

"Please sit down." He touches the bed with the palm of his hand, moves a little, and gives me some space.

"Thanks," he quietly says after I sit, reaching his hand out and holding my fingers.

"For what?" I feel my tears flowing, even though I promised myself I wouldn't cry anymore.

"I sat here in bed and listened to them, how they talk about you," he slowly says, as if searching for the words. "And I thought to myself that I fought against them, and I could fall in battle and be captured by the Germans." He is silent for a moment. "And if that were to happen, I would want a German nurse like you to take care of me."

I hold the palm of his hand tightly and press it to my teary cheeks, feeling the warmth of his fingers and holding myself back from kissing them, while still touching his fingers with my lips.

"Do you know she's waiting for me, back home, to marry me?" He doesn't move his palm.

"Yes, I know," I answer and move his hand away, releasing it and

shedding even more tears. What
else could I tell him?

I'm silent, I want to keep holding
his hand, or lie next to him on the
bed, just for a moment, but I know
I mustn't. He thinks someone is
waiting for him back home, but
the silence between us becomes
uncomfortable, it's time to say good
night.

"So now I have pilots' glasses,
and I can imagine that I'm flying?"
He finally says, and it seems he's
smiling at me.

"Yes, you have pilots' glasses."
I don't want to go upstairs to
the room I share with the other
nurses, Audrey is there. I want to
continue holding his hand, touching
my thighs. But he has Georgia,
and I have my bed waiting for

me upstairs, wrapped in an itchy, woolen military blanket with all the other nurses around. I have to be one of them. This is the place for me.

***

"You need to hurry, they're coming to pick us up soon, we're late. I need to use the mirror too."

"Do you think it's okay if I wear khakis?" I move aside and sit on my bed, watching as she stands in front of the small mirror in the room, her fingers buttoning the white dress one button at a time. My white nurse's dress is spread out on my bed, waiting for me.

"You'll stand out anyway, so it doesn't really matter." Audrey moves in front of the mirror, examining herself and making sure the dress fits to her satisfaction. "You can't go with us looking like that." She looks at me.

I've been walking around in my underwear for a long time now, trying to ignore my wooden leg while looking at myself in the mirror. I shouldn't have asked to join her tonight.

"And what does this club look like?"

"This isn't Chicago, don't set your hopes too high," she says while combing her hair, curling it fashionably. I used to do the same when I had two legs and dance clubs to go to in Chicago, when I loved myself so much, but I mustn't think about it now. I promised myself I wouldn't change my mind.

"Is it a big club?"

"They're pilots, but they live in corrugated iron huts and tents. I think you'll fit in." She's putting on her red lipstick.

"And will there be more girls there?"

"I always see more girls there, maybe from the Transportation Corps, I think they're truck drivers but I'm not sure. You can always be one of them with your faded khaki uniform," she smiles to herself in the mirror.

I look at my dress again, lying on the bed. I have to decide.

"You should put on some lipstick, that way no one will look at your feet." Audrey tosses her red lipstick tube on my bed, and I look in the mirror, trying to keep from crying.

But when she bends down to put on her shoes, I take her lipstick, approach the mirror, and put it on, applying a thick layer on my lips. Maybe everyone in the club will just look at them.

"You'd better hurry, this isn't Chicago where men are waiting on girls for a date," Audrey says to me and walks out of the room, leaving behind a trail of rose-scented perfume. I stand and watch the simple khaki uniform thrown next to the white nurse's dress. I have to decide.

"Here's Grace, who stole my sunglasses." Henry stands in the dark next to his jeep, and jokes with the girls already sitting inside the crowded vehicle, all of them lit by the dim light emanating from the hospital's front entrance. "Nice to meet you again," he watches me as I carefully go down the stairs, hoping I won't slip without the cane Francesca gave me.

"Nice to meet you again, Henry the plane driver," I smile and approach him. How am I going to take the sunglasses back from John now? "I thought you bomber pilots have everything you need, and if something's missing you write a note and get it a second later," I add, and he laughs.

"First of all, you have to teach us how to write." He gives me his hand and helps me get in the back of the jeep, huddled with the other two girls already sitting there.

"So, you finally decided to stay simple?" Audrey smiles at me when she returns to the front seat next to

Henry, after getting out and letting me get in the back with the rest. "What were you two talking about?" she asks.

"About how good the bomber pilots have it," Henry replies as he sits in the driver's seat and starts the engine. "Are you all holding on tight?" He laughs as the jeep accelerates, and I grip the metal frame so as not to fall back, placing my other hand on my khaki pants. I can't let everyone see my wooden leg.

"Is it comfortable in the back?" Henry speaks loudly, trying to overcome the engine noise.

"Very comfortable," the two other nurses crowded beside me in the back are laughing, and I laugh with them. I have to be one of them.

the door open until I reach the doorway.

"Thanks," I smile at him.

"We're not just bomber drivers. We're also gentlemen." He removes his visor and laughs, closing the door behind me.

The Squadron Officers' Club is nothing more than a simple hut made of corrugated iron, filled with loud jazz music and cigarette smoke. Some officers are standing by the wooden bar in the corner, talking to each other. A few others are sitting at the small wooden table to one side, laughing with several women. I've already seen some of the nurses and I don't know who the others are, dressed like me in khaki uniforms – maybe army drivers, as Audrey said. One couple is dancing in the center of the hut, holding each other, and when I raise my eyes, I notice the flags hanging on the hut's ceiling. The first is a US flag, next a flag with a wing painted on it, probably their squadron flag, and a torn red Nazi flag next to them.

"A trophy from North Africa, we took it from a German officers' club after they retreated. We love souvenirs," Henry explains to me as he sees me looking at the swastika flag. "Does it bother you?"

"Why would it bother me?" I step inside. Everyone thinks I love them anyway. "Aren't we all souvenir collectors?" I reply and think that I have for example collected a wooden leg called Pinocchio, but I don't tell him that.

"Come join us around our luxurious dining table," Henry accompanies me to the nurses' table, where they're all wearing white.

"Thank you, Your Highness, Prince Pilot, for bringing me to this magnificent palace," I walk to the simple wooden table. For a moment I want to join the army drivers in their khaki uniforms, sitting in the other corner. At least with them I won't stand out as much.

"Compared to the tents we sleep in, it's a magnificent house," another pilot laughs as he joins us, introducing himself and shaking my hand. "But your mansion is above all, we call it the palace," he adds while bringing me a chair and inviting me to sit.

"We're such spoiled nurses," Audrey

replies, smiling at him with her red lipstick.

"Girls, what would you like to drink?" Henry asks us as he pulls a cigarette from his jacket pocket, lighting it for himself.

"I'd love to have some whiskey," Audrey asks as she reaches for his jacket pocket. Her fingers pull out the box of cigarettes, and she also pulls out a cigarette for herself, putting it in her mouth and waiting for Henry and the other pilot to offer her a light. "Thanks," she says as she blows the smoke up and smiles at me.

"And you?" The other pilot turns to the other nurses and me.

"Gin, please," I awkwardly smile at him.

While waiting for the men to bring the drinks, I look around at the small dance floor that now has three couples on it, moving to the sound of the swing music, moving their hips and hands to the rhythm of the trumpet. I need to smile more, all the women around me look so perfect. Only the color of their hair and eyes sets them apart. We even all applied the red lipstick the same, as if it came from the same military bag.

"Here you go, girls," the men arrive and put the drinks on the table, to the sound of the other girls' laughter.

"Let's toast the nurses of the United States Army," one of the pilots who joined us raises his glass in the air.

"Let's toast our heroic pilots," the girls reply, and sip the whiskey.

"May the war and the beautiful nurses go on forever," Henry smiles at all the girls at the table, drinking his whisky.

"May you continue bombing German cities and destroy them," Audrey replies and raises her glass in the air, and everyone joins.

"Let's toast the planes that guard us," he says.

"Let's toast the ambulances that bring us the wounded so we can take care of them." She picks up the drink in her hand and smiles at him, and I turn my gaze away from them and look at the couples on the small dance floor. I have to imagine I'm one of them.

"How were you injured?" Henry yells at me from the other side of the table, trying to overcome the music.

"What's it like to fly?" I ask back and empty my glass of gin in one gulp, feeling the heat of the drink in my throat.

"Flying's like a dream." He leans in my direction while one of the girls puts her arm on his shoulder, and all the girls watch his lips as he talks to me. "The plane takes off, and at that moment you feel like a bird, you see everything from above, clearer, sharper. And everything looks smaller, like you're a giant looking at the world from the clouds. Want a cigarette?" He pulls out the box of cigarettes and offers me one, and I notice Audrey and the other girls looking.

"No thanks," I smile at him and make sure to smile at the other pilots listening to us as well, as I move my body slightly to the beat of the music, trying to sip from the empty glass again, imagining that I'm dancing.

"And then," Henry continues to talk to me and the other girls, leaning back and spreading his hands to the sound of the girls laughing. "And then you feel how small we all are, and how big and amazing this world is. It's just you and the noise of the engines destroying the peaceful silence around." He looks at the other girls, smiles at Audrey, and they all smile back at him. "And of course, my co-pilot George destroys the silence by telling me bad jokes on my headphones, even when the Germans are shooting at us with their anti-aircraft cannons." He points to one of the pilots standing by the bar, and all the girls look at him. "George, come join us," he yells. "There are beautiful women here who want to meet you." And George smiles at us, bringing a chair and joining the table crowded with nurses and pilots.

"Another gin," one of the pilots hands me a glass, and I smile at him and take the drink from his outstretched hand, even though I didn't ask for it.

"Would you like to dance?" he asks me.

"No thank you, I don't like to dance, but you can go invite someone else." I look at the other nurses at the table. It seems to me that they're eager to dance. The lipstick tastes strange to me mixed with the taste of the gin.

"I'll dance with you." Audrey gets up and holds his hand as she smiles at Henry, and we all watch them as they turn their backs to us, stepping onto the small dance floor.

A new song begins, and Audrey and the pilot dance and wave their hands in the air, touching and holding each other as they swing together, until his hands grip her waist while he spins her in the air. Despite the loud music, I can hear her laughter, her hands on his shoulders while everyone looks at their moves and cheers, until the song is over. They're both standing in the center, laughing and panting, while she smiles at Henry.

"Audrey sure knows how to dance," Henry says to me during the applause.

"Yes, she sure knows how to make the right moves." I also used to know how to make those moves.

Two more women join her in the center of the hut, expelling the men from the dance floor and standing in a line. They start dancing to the sound of a new song and try to move at a steady pace, looking at each other to coordinate their feet and smiling at the men around them.

"Bravo," everyone shouts and applauds them as they stand and bow to the small crowd, hugging each other before returning to our table, panting, and smiling.

"Bravo," Henry raises his glass. "You dance wonderfully." And we all raise our glasses to toast Audrey, who turns her gaze around and smiles at the pilots.

"A toast to the war that brought us together," Henry raises his glass again.

"To the war." We all drink, and I bring the second glass to my lips too, even though it's already empty.

The music turns quiet, and a few more couples fill the small dance floor, hugging each other while moving slowly, leaving the tables around me abandoned. I'm the only one left sitting, watching them, politely refusing when another pilot approaches and asks me to dance, occasionally sipping from the drinks left on the table even though they're not mine. I'll never be able to be one of them.

"Can you take me back to the

hospital?" I finally get up from the table and turn to a pilot standing at the bar. I have to ask someone.

"Are you okay?" He keeps holding the whiskey glass in his hand.

"Yeah, I'm sorry, I just don't feel well." At least I tried to be one of them.

"I'll take her," Henry leaves the girl he's dancing with and holds my hand.

"No thanks, I'll manage. I think I drank too much." I don't want him to feel sorry for me. I saw him dancing with Audrey before dancing with this girl, hugging each other and whispering. She's probably already told him about my leg.

"It's okay," he says, still holding my hand.

"You're dancing with a girl," I look at him.

"I'll be back soon." He strokes the girl's shoulder and whispers something in her ear that makes her smile at him before he turns to the door with me. If he takes me and hurries back, maybe he'll still have time for another slow dance with her.

We walk side by side to the jeep, and I try to stay steady, lowering my gaze so I don't stumble. He should've danced with his girl now, not pity me. He could laugh and hold her in his arms, spin her in the air.

"Thanks." I let him hold my hand as I climb into the jeep, watching him get into the driver's seat and start the engine. Why did he volunteer to take me, leaving that beautiful girl he was dancing with? But he says nothing as we start driving in the dark, and the jeep lights are the only visible thing on the dirt tracks of the airfield.

"I want to show you something," he finally says, raising his voice to overcome the engine noise as he changes direction to another dirt road, and we begin passing by the heavy bombers. They stand dark in the night, in an endless line, like good-natured whales patiently resting on the ground, waiting for the morning to come so they can be loaded with heavy bombs and make their way towards the enemy.

One, two, three, four, I quietly count them, but soon lose count and just watch their silhouettes; another and another, they don't stop appearing in the jeep's lights for a second before they disappear in the dark again, until he stops next to one of them. Henry turns the engine and car lights off. "Come with me." He gets out of the jeep and gives me his hand.

The sound of our footsteps in the dirt is the only thing heard as we slowly walk towards the dark plane, and in the moonlight, I look up at the huge wings and the large propeller engines hanging on them. The cockpit shimmers in the moonlight, and the machineguns stand out from the bright plexiglass canopies, as if they were black sticks facing the dark sky.

"Come closer," Henry says again and approaches the plane, stroking the metal, and I do the same, feeling the smooth, cold fuselage.

"Is this your plane?"

"Yes, this is my plane."

"Do you like flying?"

"It's the most wonderful feeling in the world, but you already know that; you asked me before, when we were sitting inside the hut, now I can ask you something?"

I'm silent, knowing what he's going to ask me. "Yes," I finally reply.

"How were you injured?"

"A plane shot at me." I don't want to tell him anything more.

"So, I guess you don't like pilots," he chuckles.

"I try not to be afraid of them," I smile at him.

"Are you scared of me?"

"You don't look scary to me," I look up at him. Even in the dark I can see that he is handsome. "It seems to me there are a lot of girls who aren't afraid of you."

"We're just enjoying ourselves at the club. They want to collect some pleasant moments, as we all do."

"Yes, we're all collecting pleasant moments in this war." I want to tell him that I haven't had any pleasant moments since I arrived here, but I say nothing. Maybe I'm collecting things too. My hand feels the smooth metal fuselage, and I think of John's lighter in my shirt pocket and Henry's sunglasses, which he'll never get back.

"We're at war," he finally says.
"There's enough fear around us for
a lifetime." He keeps talking, and
for a moment I think that if I were
Audrey, I could stroke him now,
tell him that war sometimes hurts
your body and your soul. But I'm
not Audrey or one of the other girls
waiting for him, and I keep stroking
the side of the cold plane, running
my fingers over it.

"And aren't you afraid of flying
towards Germany?"

"I can't allow myself to be afraid.
This is why I came here, to win this
war. If we don't do this job, no one
else will."

"Yes, you're right. You can't be
afraid." I look at him. We all mustn't
be afraid. We're at war.

"This banishes my fears." He takes something out of his jacket pocket, and I see his face in the faint moonlight, smell the leather scent of his pilot's jacket.

"What is it?" I reach out and feel the small, flat metal whiskey flask.

"This is my mascot. This is my guardian angel of whiskey."

"Your mascot?"

"To overcome the fear." He sips from the small bottle and offers it to me, but I refuse; I've already drunk too much. "I got it from the previous captain of this plane," he keeps on saying.

"And what happened to him?"

"He flew too much," he quietly laughs.

"And what's this?" I run my hand over the fuselage. There's something painted on it.

Henry pulls a lighter out of his jacket pocket and lights it, bringing the flame closer to the fuselage, and I notice a drawing of a girl painted on the plane's nose. She's lying in a seductive pose, wearing a red swimsuit and a perfect smile, with her hair painted in waves of blond, spilling over the name 'Betty,' written in rounded letters. A row of bombs and three swastikas are next to her almost-naked body.

"Is she watching over you too?" I turn to him, watching his face in the light of the faint lighter flame.

"Do you see the swastikas?" His hand rises and brings the lighter closer to the three curved crosses painted in black on the silver plane's body. "Every time we fly, their fighter planes try to kill us," he continues while I remain silent. "This is when we managed to kill them. So yes, she's probably also watching over me." His hand holding the lighter passes over the girl's drawing in the red swimsuit, while I reach out and touch the black-painted swastikas with my fingertip.

"Do you have someone waiting for you back home?" He turns off the lighter, and we both return to the darkness, with only the moonlight above us.

"No, I don't have anyone. And you? Do you have a girl waiting for you?"

"No girl is waiting for me."

"So, who do you belong to?" I

think of the women in the club who wonder where he's gone. Why did he bring me here?

"I don't belong to anyone."

"Except Betty, who's guarding you?" I lay my hand on the drawing of the girl in the red swimsuit.

"Do you smoke?" Henry asks as he pulls out a box of cigarettes and lights one for himself.

"No, I don't smoke."

"We're moving from one place to another, she's far away, and I'm far away, and I keep her close to me, drawn on the plane I use for fighting, but we're at war," he quietly says, and I can barely see his lips in the dark. "You and I, and everyone in this damn war, move from one place to another. We are

53

all war wanderers." The cigarette momentarily lights his face as he inhales from it.

"You're right." I extend my fingers and feel my way to his jacket pocket, feel the soft leather and pull out the box of cigarettes and the lighter. Henry says nothing at the touch of my hands wandering over his body. In the dark it seems like he's smiling as I put a cigarette between my lips and light it, momentarily seeing my fingers lit by the lighter as he also sends out his hand to wrap around mine, protecting the flame from the soft evening breeze. "You're right," I say again and exhale the smoke into the cool sky. "We're war wanderers." Above me, in the dim light of the cigarette and the moon, I notice Betty's flowing hair painted on the nose of the plane.

We both stand in the dark and smoke in silence under the shadow of the bomber, as if knowing what's going to happen in a few minutes. I count the cigarette inhalations, but I can't be like the other girls, even though I know I should. The lipstick is weird to me, and my leg bothers me. All I can think about now is John, even though I don't have to think about him; he believes he has his Georgia waiting for him back home.

"Will you please take me back?" I step away from him and breathe the night air, touching the cold metal of the plane.

"Yes, of course." It takes Henry a few seconds to answer while standing in the dark, watching me, and I hope he doesn't try to kiss me. What will happen after the kiss?

Will he dance with me after finding out I'm disabled? What would he say if he knew about the wooden leg?

"I apologize," I say as he walks to the jeep, and I follow him, climbing into the vehicle and sitting next to him. This time he doesn't offer me his hand.

"It's okay. I just wanted to ask how you got injured. I thought you'd like to talk about it."

I don't believe him, but I'm happy for the jeep engine noise and the wind during the ride, which eases the silence between us as we pass through the dark village on our way back to the hospital.

"Good night. I had a pleasant evening." He politely kisses my cheek as I get out of the jeep, and we say goodbye at the hospital's driveway next to the huge Red Cross flag spread out on the ground, barely visible by the moonlight.

"I had a pleasant evening too, thank you," I smile at him and turn my back to the jeep, walking as upright as I can and hearing the noise of the jeep receding on the gravel. He has to hurry, one of the girls is waiting for him at the club.

I sit on the hospital stairs and look at the night outside. I can still hear the jeep's engine moving away and see its lights in the distance, like two small streaks of light in the dark.

My hand grips Henry's lighter, which I didn't return, and I compare the engraving on it to John's lighter. Is this my destiny? Will I never dance again? To always sit and watch other girls be hugged by handsome men? Will I always live in fear that someone will find out about my leg at the end of the evening? Will I sit alone on the hospital stairs?

I toss the cigarette and get up. I have to do something.

***

"John, get up." I touch his shoulder.

"John, get up." I reach my hand out again, stroking his hair.

"Gracie?"

"Yeah, it's me," I smile. At least he didn't mention my limp. "John, get up."

"Gracie, are you drunk?"

"Not enough," I grab his shirt, trying to lift him into a sitting position.

"It seems to me it was much more than enough. You smell of gin."

"I like gin," I whisper to him. "John, I need you to come with me."

"Gracie, what time is it?"

"It's the middle of the night outside, but it doesn't matter. I need you to come with me." I pull his hand. Maybe I drank a little too much.

"Where to?" He sits on the bed.

"Somewhere, to do something; take me to the beach."

"We can't go to the beach; you're drunk and I'm blind."

"Please, John." It seems to me that I'm starting to cry. "I have to do something."

"What happened?" He searches and places his hand on mine.

"This war happened," I whisper to him while his warm hands stroke my fingers, and I want him to continue. I no longer care to stay here by his bed all night, I just need him to caress me like that until I fall asleep.

"Let's go," he says after a while, pulling his warm fingers away from my hand. He gets out of bed, placing his hand on my shoulder. We quietly leave the hall of the wounded, careful not to make noise and draw the night nurse's attention; she's sitting in her tiny room reading a book.

The hospital garden is dark, and I walk towards the cliff and the path leading down the beach, even though I know I'm not supposed to and that I'm unsteady. I can feel John's hand resting on my shoulder, letting me guide him, but it seems to me that sometimes he holds me so that I don't fall, until I no longer know whether he's following me or if I'm leaning on his arm.

"Gracie, are you okay?"

"'I've been okay for six months. A few more steps, we're close."

"To the beach?"

"To go down to the shore." I can already hear the sound of the waves crashing against the rocks at the bottom of the cliff, but I feel John's hand tighten on my shoulders.

"I think we'll stop here." He holds me back.

"A few more steps, we've almost arrived at the path."

"I think we'll stay here." He holds my arm and prevents me from walking further.

"John, the beach is waiting for us." I get my arm free, grab his hand and try to pull him after me. There are only a few more steps before we can go down the path. It's somewhere here, even though I don't see it in the dark. I know it's there. If I can only find it, we can go down the cliff and the beach. I need the sea; the waves are calling to me. But John holds me tightly and doesn't let me move any further, his hand wrapped around my body, shaking from the cool night breeze.

"Please, John. I have to do something." I turn to him and place my hands on his shoulders. "Let's dance, like we danced then, on the road." I try to move my body to the beat of imaginary music, start humming in a whisper, as we did that time.

"Gracie, what happened?"

"I'm full of lies, John. I'm a liar." I let go of him and bend to the ground, clinging to his legs so as not to fall, and whimper as I hit the grass.

"Gracie, what lies?" He bends over me, touching my pulled-up hair.

"I've lied to you," I start to cry. "John, I don't have a leg, I don't have a leg." I lay down on the grass and look at the dark sky. "I wasn't just injured, I lost my leg, it was amputated." I whimper, feeling his fingers caressing my hair. It seems that he's sitting down next to me on the grass.

"A German plane shot me, and I'm disabled. I'll never recover. I'll never dance again. I'll always be disabled," I cry and look at the stars twinkling in the sky, but maybe it's because of my tears.

"Sh... it's okay..." he continues to stroke my hair.

"What will I do?" I keep crying,

hating myself so much for breaking down again. "Everyone is watching me all the time, staring at me, the limp girl with the wooden leg."

"Then you'll have to learn to be Grace again." His hand keeps stroking my hair and shoulders.

"I can't learn to be myself again. It doesn't pass, it'll never pass, the pain, the looks around me, the pity."

"I don't pity you." He keeps stroking my cheeks, and I want to tell him it's because he can't see how ugly I am.

"Because you're injured too." I don't wipe my tears away.

"Yes, because I'm injured too, and it won't pass for me either."

"So come with me to the beach,

let's go together." I look away from the cliff into the dark, where I can hear the waves of the sea. Maybe we can both walk there.

"We'll stay here together." I feel the touch of his hand as he hugs me. His fingers are warm on my quivering body.

"I can no longer be so different, hiding myself so much, trying to imagine what they're thinking of me."

"Why does what they think of you matters to you?" He hugs me tightly.

"Because you don't see their looks."

"That's true, I really can't see their looks."

"John, I'm sorry, I didn't mean

that." I start crying again. "You're the only one who doesn't feel sorry for me."

"Because of your amputated leg?"

"Yes," I nod my head, even though he can't see it.

"Can I feel it?"

"My leg?" I turn my gaze to him.

"Yes, can I?"

I try to examine the expression on his face, but I fail to do so in the dark.

With both my hands, I pull my khaki pant leg upwards, lifting it above my knee, then I hold his hand and guide it to my stump, placing his fingers on my prosthetic leg.

With our hands held together, I slowly let him feel the smooth wooden prosthetic leg, down to my shoe and then back towards my knee and thighs. I feel his fingers caress the strips of leather that tie the stump to my leg.

"What is it?"

"These are leather straps. They tie the wooden leg in place, so it doesn't slip, and stays stable." I stay lying down, looking at the stars, not daring to look at him.

"And is it comfortable?"

"I have to get used to it, and sometimes it hurts. I also can't walk with it for a long time because the wound is still sensitive, but it's kind of a leg, better than nothing." For a moment I want to take off the wooden leg and let him feel the stump, but I don't have the courage.

"Your leg is like Pinocchio, who wants to be a real boy," he whispers and continues to caress the strips of leather that harness my leg.

"Yes, like Pinocchio the liar." I keep looking at the sky. I also have no courage to tell him the truth about the woman he loves.

"You're not the only one who hides things and lies." He stops stroking my leg after a while and leans back. "I hide things too." I turn my gaze to him.

"I lie to her. Can you help me write a letter to Georgia and tell her?"

John bends over the small metal locker by his bed, looking for a candle, and I put my hand on his shoulder and look around the dark hall. All the wounded soldiers are asleep, and the shift nurse is sitting in her room. How can I write a letter to Georgia?

"Do you have a light? I had a lighter in my bag, but I lost it," he asks me as he gets up and gives me a candle. "It must've fallen off when I was injured in Florence or when I was evacuated here." I tuck my hand into my pocket, feeling his lighter beside Henry's. I have to give them back; I'm both a liar and a thief.

"Why do you have a lighter? Do you smoke? You don't smoke." I light the candle, placing it on his locker. I'll find a way to return the lighter to him.

"No, I don't smoke." He sits in his bed. "The lighter isn't mine."

"So, whose is it?"

"It belongs to Private Robert Walker of Iowa, who dreamed of growing corn like his father," he whispers into the dark. "Shall we write the letter?"

"Wait a minute," I say. "I'll be right back." I get up, hurry to my room, and take my pad, the one I never use to write any letters.

"I'm ready," I say to him a few minutes later, sitting down on the edge of his bed, holding the pad and pen in my hand. I'll write the letter and not send it; it won't matter to John anyway.

"He gave me the lighter when we were on the landing craft, a few minutes before we stormed the beach at Anzio, when we were all shaking with fear," he quietly says, and I put my hand in the pocket of my uniform and feel it.

"This was our third landing, after Tunisia and Sicily," he continues. "And we were already really scared, we felt twice as lucky, and this time it wouldn't happen again. He was with me from the beginning, when we joined the army in 1941, right after Pearl Harbor. He slept on the bed next to mine at boot camp." John holds my hand in the dark. "And that's it. He gave me the lighter for luck, even though I didn't want to take it from him. There was an engraving on it, To Hell and Back, that he somehow managed to engrave. Maybe he found some engraver in the nearby Sicilian village when we prepared for the invasion of Anzio. In the boat he told me he felt he'd made a mistake and that the lighter would bring him bad luck from now on. He asked me to take it, so that at least one of us would return from the beach alive." John stops talking but keeps holding my hand tightly until I feel pain in my fingers, but I don't move my hand.

"You know," he continues after a while, "on stories, we always expect some dramatic ending, like in the movies, with music in the background or some wonderful ending sentence, but there was nothing." He releases his grip, and I stroke his trembling fingers. "One moment we're running between the houses in Anzio, storming a German bunker, and that's it, a moment later he was no more; such shitty luck." I think I can see tears streaming down his cheeks in the dark. "I kept wanting to return the lighter to him, to tell him it's damn bad luck to visit Hell in Anzio, but I couldn't." His hand trembles on the blanket, and I hold it tightly. "Then we had to keep fighting, moving forward, and they took him. I wanted to go back to him, give him back his lighter, but there are places you can't go back to, like that place – Anzio." I wipe the tears from my eyes, hoping he doesn't notice.

"Don't cry," he says. "It's just a silly story about a lousy lighter. Maybe it's better that it's lost."

"Let's write your loved one a happy letter, not something sad," I say. "She loves you and is waiting for you back home."

"I can't. I tell you stories that make you cry so as to not write that letter. I'm a coward."

"You're not a coward." I want to hug him, knowing I'm much more cowardly than he is.

"You're a woman, can you perhaps write to her and tell her what happened to me? So, it'll be less painful?"

"Yes, I'm a woman," I say, even though I don't feel like a woman. I'm a coward and a liar Pinocchio doll with a wooden leg.

***

"Hey, wooden leg, come help me," she calls me the next day, and I follow her to the driveway, walking behind her to the truck parked at the entrance. "We have a shipment from Naples. We need to get it inside." She walks to the back of the truck and removes the green tarp cover, revealing small wooden crates marked with seals.

"What are those?"

"Medicine, Gracie. The kind that made you so feel so good when you were on the wounded side, lying in your white bed and whimpering in pain." She grabs one of the crates and throws it at me, and I hurry to grab it, even though I almost stumble. "Blanche decided I should help with the interns' dirty work." She also grabs one of the crates and takes it off the truck, walking into the building. "Blanche must feel sorry for you."

"Why do you hate me?" I stay, standing and looking at her, holding the wooden box.

"I don't hate you, Gracie." She keeps walking, and I start following her, grabbing the crate, and trying not to stumble as I climb the stairs.

"Yes, you hate me. Once I thought we could be friends."

"We can't be friends." She keeps walking and places the box in the corner of the little medicine room.

"Even though you don't like me, we can try and be friends. You helped me when I was injured, and I helped you with the German." I place the crate I brought on top of hers.

"You didn't help me with the German." She turns to me and brings her lips closer to mine. "You did him a favor and left him alive. If he wants, he can thank you." And she turns and walks away from me, out to the truck parked outside.

"So, I didn't help you. You just helped me," I follow her, not telling her that he already thanked me on the wall in my corner. I need to erase what he engraved.

"Exactly." She takes another crate from the trunk. "And we can't even be close to calling ourselves friends."

"Why?" I'm holding another crate, like her.

"I'm too veteran in this business, and you're too young, we can never be friends. You wouldn't understand."

"What wouldn't I understand?"

"I've been wandering in this war for three years." She walks ahead of me. "You have no idea what three years means."

I walk after her and want to tell her that even a few months are enough in this place, but she stops again and turns to me.

"Do you receive letters from home?" She looks into my eyes.

The letters to John, did she see them in my locker? Is she rummaging through my things? Or does she remember the time I told her I have someone back home? I must return the letters to him.

"Yes, I do receive letters from home." I look back at her. What does she know?

"I no longer receive letters, no one still writes to anyone after three years." She keeps walking, holding the crate in her hands. "And that's okay, it makes sense that this happens, the difference between us is that you still think it won't happen to you."

"Letters are not the most important thing in the world." Sometimes at night, I sit and read Georgia's letters, trying to imagine what John would've written to her.

"You have someone waiting for you back home, I no longer have anyone, but I don't care." She places the crate in the small cubicle and turns to the truck again, and I follow her. I shouldn't have told her that I had someone.

"Audrey, where are you from?"

"From New York. Why does it matter?" She collects a new crate. "I'm from North Africa, from Morocco, from Casablanca, from Kasserine Pass, from Sicily, from Italy, I'm from the war."

"I was in New York, albeit only for a few hours," I reply. "On the way here, I didn't get to see the city, I just passed through Grand Central Station, and I was in Italy. I was in some other places too, I'm not young and naïve." I struggle with the heavy wooden crate. My leg hurts.

"'I was in New York'," she imitates me. "You're like a woman who's never been with a man and wants someone to love her. Just so you know, I hate New York and Grand Central Station, there are seven million people in that city, and everyone passes by that station without smiling to each other once. It's a city of lonely people."

"And none of them are waiting for you?" I'll never tell her that I've never been with a man.

"It's none of your business, wooden leg. I asked for help carrying crates, not for you to ask me about my private life and not for you to be my friend." She takes another box. "And to be honest, you have to do this job, not me. This is the new one's job." She puts the box back in the trunk. "You can keep unloading the truck. You wanted to be a nurse, didn't you?" She stands aside and lights a cigarette for herself.

"Yeah, I wanted to be a nurse." I grab the crate she put in the back of the truck, ignoring my sore leg, and start walking to the medicine room. I won't let her mock me anymore.

"Don't try to be my friend. You'll never succeed," she says as I go back to get another crate.

"You don't have to be in this war for three years to understand it. You made that very clear," I reply and take another one, ignoring my sweat.

"Okay, Gracie, don't be offended." She tosses the cigarette and comes to help me with the crates. "We'll be friends if you want it that much."

But even though I smile at her, I don't believe her.

***

"Gracie, you should join us too. Don't you want to be one of us?" She turns to me a few days later as I enter our bedroom after my shift is over. She's standing in the center of the room, trying on a yellow dress. "It's nice out there. There won't be many more days like this before winter." She looks at herself in the mirror. "Join us. No one cares if you come in your simple khaki uniform."

"And where are you going?" Does she want to make fun of me again?

"Why do you care where? Just be thankful for being invited." She lets her hair down and combs it.

"Who else is coming?"

"Your Henry's coming," she smiles at her figure in the mirror. "And a few more pilots too."

"Henry isn't mine."

"I was wondering why you let him take you back that evening."

"I didn't want to, he insisted."

"I thought you had someone waiting for you back home." She examines herself, spinning around.

"Yes, I have someone waiting for me back home." I sit down on my bed, sorry I lied to her that time, but I can't back out now.

"I'm waiting for them outside with the other girls. You'd better hurry up. No one's going to wait for you." She finishes combing her hair and throws me her red lipstick. I stay sitting on the bed and look at the lipstick laying on the woolen military blanket.

I need to fit in. I also need to wear red lipstick so that no one looks at my limp or my khaki uniform. My leg is too ugly for me to wear dresses.

A pleasant autumn noon sun warms the stairs of the hospital's entrance, and the other girls are already sitting on them in colorful dresses, looking at the road leading to the hospital entrance, waiting for the pilots.

"At least I look like the stalk among all the flowers, I belong too," I whisper to myself as I exit the main entrance towards them. I sit a few feet away, enjoying looking at them from the side. They're so beautiful as they chat and look at the main road in anticipation.

Like the gurgling noise of smug cats, three jeeps emerge behind the bend of the main road and enter the mansion's gate, stopping in front of the girls, who go down the stairs and walk towards them, spreading out like colorful petals.

"Good morning, girls. Our convoy is about to leave soon," I think I hear Henry's voice among all the pilots laughing and hugging the petal girls. Although I'm advancing towards him, by the time I get to his jeep it's already full of girls, and Henry is busy bowing and talking to one of them. I turn to the last jeep in the convoy and step inside. It doesn't really matter to me anyway. He was nice to me that evening out of politeness.

"Nice to meet you," the pilot who huddles with me in the back of the jeep introduces himself, and I smile at him, shaking his hand.

"Are you a nurse too?" he asks as the jeep starts moving, looking at my uniform.

"No, I'm just an intern," I reply. "And intern nurses aren't allowed to wear white dresses. I'm hardly allowed to measure blood pressure for the wounded." It seems to me that if he wanted to hold my hand before, he's changed his mind.

We stayed completely silent for the rest of the drive, looking at the nurse sitting in the front seat, how she laughs with her pilot and places her hand on the back of his neck, stroking his short hair. I think the pilot next to me in the back of the jeep is sorry he only got an intern nurse. I should be nice to him.

"Where are we going?" I ask and smile at him, wearing Audrey's red lipstick.

"Haven't you been told?" he asks. "We found a lovely sandy bay on the seashore, so we decided to invite you for a picnic." He smiles back at me and almost holds my hand.

"I love the beach." I look out of the jeep and think it would've been nice if Audrey had told me where we were going.

"It's probably hard to be the new one with all the veteran nurses."

"No, they're nice to me."

"I'm sure you'll have fun at the beach."

"I'm sure I will." I think of the soft sand and smile at him, forcing myself to place the palm of my hand on his arm. I must learn to fit in.

The jeeps go down to the bay and stop at the end of the dirt road, and I look out to the shore and the distant sea. The water is clear turquoise, and the sandy beach strip is empty and clean, as if inviting us to walk on it. But not me, I can't walk on the soft sand with my prosthetic leg.

"Let's go to the sea, lovely girls," Henry's voice roars. "The last one to reach the water's edge is making coffee for everyone." The girls hurry out of the vehicles, taking off their shoes and running on the soft sand while laughing.

"Here you are, the girl in khaki,"

Henry approaches me as I get out of the jeep and stand, looking at them running ahead of me. "I thought I saw you when we arrived earlier, but you disappeared."

"I chose someone else. Your truck was already full of lovely girls."

"I always have room in my truck," he bows and kisses my hand chivalrously. "Though you chose excellently." He taps the shoulder of the pilot standing next to me, unpacking blankets, and a picnic basket from the jeep. "'Aren't you competing? I think you'll have to make us all coffee. "

I look at the impossible strip of sand and the distant sea. Audrey and the other girls have already reached the water, walking barefoot between the waves, splashing on the sand. What can I tell him to sound funny and not make him suspect that I can't walk in this place?

"Are you coming?" the other pilot asks, starts walking towards the others.

"I'm sorry, I have to stay here. I'm not feeling well, feminine issues," I finally say to Henry, knowing it's not as funny as I wanted it to be. "I'll stay here to keep an eye on the jeeps for you."

"Are you sure?" Henry looks at me. "There's no one here except a few seagulls, and what will they steal from the jeeps, our sunglasses?"

"Yes, I'm sure I'll stay here and watch the jeeps. Go join them, they're waiting for you." I look at Audrey and another of the nurses, standing and watching us. "I'll wait for you all in the jeep. I'm having fun here."

"Are you sure?" he asks again. "The sea is still warm this time of the year."

"Yes, I'm sure." I want him to go already, so he won't notice the tears on the sides of my face and pity me.

He smiles and touches my arm for a second, before he turns his back and runs to join his friends, taking off his military-issue shirt while I look at his muscular back, as he goes to talk to the other girl. I turn my face away from them and wipe my tears.

"I'm sorry, I'm not feeling well. I have some feminine issues," I whisper contemptuously to myself as I sit by the driver's seat of the silent jeep, playing with the steering wheel and trying to press the pedals with my wooden leg. "I definitely found an amusing sentence. I'm the amusing nurse everyone feels sorry for."

"I'm actually a Transport Corps driver, I'm here at the beach by mistake," I talk to a convoy of ants transporting wheat grains to their underground nest.

"I patiently wait for them to finish having fun," I explain to the nail I hold in my hand, using it to engrave the side of the jeep.

"I need something to hide my Pinocchio leg, so I can wear a dress," I whisper to the distant sea and the group of women and men

sitting on the water's edge, laughing
and splashing water on each other.
I can never be one of them if I can't
hide my wooden leg.

12. The Voyage to Rome.

"Americana, we're at war, he says he doesn't have enough leather for boots, certainly not for a boot as tall as you want," she turns around and says to me.

We're both inside the shoemaker's small shop in the village square, surrounded by the scent of leather, shoe polish, and wooden shoe forms that hang on the walls in pairs, with names engraved on them, probably those of all the villagers.

"Americana," he walks over and hugs me as I enter his store, a few minutes before, following Francesca and looking around at all the tools spread on his small wooden table. But since then, He and Francesca have been arguing and pointing at my leg. I look at them and occasionally turn my head to see if the kids peek out the window again. But this time, the filthy glass is empty of their smiling faces. The falling rain must've driven them away.

"All the leather went to the army, to the soldiers' shoes," she tells me. "He says it's impossible to get leather these days."

"Rome," he says to her. "Rome." And she turns around and argues with him again.

"What is he saying?"

"He says he hates Rome," she turns to me.

"So why is he mentioning Rome?"

"Because in Rome, there are the luxury shops that he hates, the ones that never care if there is a war in the world, they always have nice leather."

"Does a pair of boots there cost a lot of money?"

"Americana, don't you understand that you are an Americana? With your cigarettes, you can buy whatever you want here, so with your money, you can buy even more of whatever you want."

"Americana, Rome," the shoemaker smiles at me, and I take out the box of cigarettes I brought especially for him, placing it in his hand, but he refuses to take it, even though I insist.

"I'm not going with you to Rome,"

Francesca snatches the cigarette box from my hand, places it on his desk, grabs my hand, and pulls me out of the shop.

"Why won't you go to Rome?"

"Because I hate that city, and I'm not going away from my child," she walks to her motorcycle, which is standing in the square, wet from the rain.

"Do you have a child?" I stand and watch her. Why didn't she tell me?

"Yes, Americana, I have a child," she turns to me.

"And why didn't you tell me you had a child?"

"Because you don't know everything, Americana," she turns her back and continues walking towards her motorcycle.

"How old is your child?"

"What are you implying?" She turns to me again, her hair wild and fluttering.

"I'm not implying anything."

"Do you want to know who the father is? Do you think I was like all those women who met German soldiers after my husband disappeared in Russia? Impressed by their glittering ranks?" She raises her voice.

"No, Francesca, I don't think that."

"I had one husband, and I hated his uniform, and I hate the Germans. When he would come back home on vacation, I wanted to cut his uniform to pieces and throw them into the fire," she turns away from me and starts walking. "And my name is not Francesca, my name is the widow with the motorcycle."

"Francesca, I don't think that. Will you let me meet your child?" I follow her and raise my voice.

"No."

"Why not?"

"Because you're Americana, who understands nothing, and wants to go to Rome."

"Then I'll go there with someone else."

"It's exactly what you should do," she lifts her black dress and presses it to her thighs, before sitting on the motorcycle's wet seat, dripping with rain. "You should find an American soldier like you, who'll take you to Rome, and you'll be lovey-dovey in front of the Colosseum."

***

"I apologize," he tells me a few days later, when I go out to the hospital's front driveway. He leans against his jeep and holds a small bouquet in his hand.

"What exactly are you apologizing for?" I look at the flowers. He must've picked them on the way, stopped by one of the bougainvillea bushes at the entrance to the hospital, the ones that climb the giant cypresses.

"About last time, we went to the sea, leaving you alone in the jeep."

"It's okay. It didn't bother me at all," I'm turning my back to him and stepping back into the hospital, I have a lot of work to do.

"Grace," Henry runs and catches up to me, touching my shoulder. "I really apologize," he hands me the bouquet of bougainvillea flowers, which are sprinkled with purple petals, on the hospital stairs. "I know you think I don't care and that I had fun on the beach with the other girls while you sat alone," he takes the palm of my hand and places the flowers in it. "I was insensitive. A gentleman shouldn't behave like that. I should've stayed with you in the jeep," he gently closes my fingers on the stems with his palm.

"I hate the beach. If I'd known you were inviting me to the beach, I wouldn't have come." I hold the flowers in my hand, wondering if he and Audrey have a new idea for humiliating me. A few minutes ago, she came and told me that someone was waiting for me outside, refusing to say who it was.

"I didn't know you hated the beach," he smiles through his new sunglasses. "Come with me, join me for a trip, just you and me."

"Thanks, but I'm busy," I turn to the entrance. I've already heard about these trips. The nurses tend to giggle about them in our room at night, telling each other what the pilots are trying to do and where they're reaching their hands when they invite them on these trips.

"Grace, I brought things for a picnic. I won't try anything, I promise."

"Why me?" I turn to him. "There are so many nurses here who'd be happy to go out with you."

"I don't know," he takes off his sunglasses and looks at me, and I take one step towards him, examining his brown eyes.

"Who does?" I look at him. Does he feel sorry for me?

"No one knows. We're at war. This isn't the time to ask tough questions, especially when a nice guy like me offers a lovely lady like you a picnic in the open air. Come with me, a little escape from this hospital," he smiles at me and bends down to the floor, collects some of the bougainvillea petals that have fallen on the stairs, and attaches them to the bouquet I'm holding, wrapping my hands. "You lost some of your flowers."

"It's because you're a bad suitor and don't know which flowers to bring a girl."

"Will you teach me?" He keeps smiling at me, his brown eyes sparkling.

"And you won't try anything?" I examine his face.

Henry bows and removes his visor, holding it with his stretched hand. "Would you be willing to join me in my carriage jeep?"

And I go downstairs, stop for a moment, look at my shoes and the limp leg covered by my khaki pants, and walk to his carriage. If I want to be like them, I must learn to fit in.

"Can I pour you some orange juice or wine?" He asks later, as we sit on a blanket spread out in a field by the side of the road, and I nod. Henry pours some orange powder into the metal cups, filled with water, from the military canteen he brought, mixes them, and hands me one.

"Thanks," I smile at him.

"Can I offer you a small reinforcement?" He smiles at me as he pulls out his small whiskey flask, and I nod my head again as he pours some for both of us, sipping his drink and leaning back, looking at the blue autumn sky.

"So, why me?" I look at him and all the food he has spread on the blanket. Such a picnic will win any girl's heart.

"Does it matter?" He laughs. "We are two people who barely know each other, sitting on a brown military wool blanket in a field of weeds and crickets in Italy, during this never-ending war. Do we have to look for logic and reasons in what we are doing?"

"You're right," I reach for his whiskey bottle, which rests on the blanket, and pours more of it into my synthetic orange juice. "We shouldn't look for reasons."

"And besides," he speaks to the sky and points to a flock of migrating birds passing south. "You can always get up and run away with the jeep if you don't like my behavior."

"Not really," I follow the birds in the sky with my eyes. "Did you forget I injured my leg?" I don't want to tell him I can't drive. Dad didn't have money to buy us a car. Back home, in Chicago, we never had enough money.

"Do you know how to drive?"

"A little," I drink more of the reinforced orange juice.

"Let's go," he gets up and holds my hand, lifts me up until I almost fall, and must hold onto him to support myself, placing my hands on his hips. "Let's see how fast you can drive."

"I'm not driving with you," I follow him to the jeep and rest my hand on the metal frame of the jeeps' window. I must tell him I can't drive at all.

"I promise not to look," he laughs, pulls me to the driver's seat, and stands beside me.

"What about all the food and the picnic blanket?" I look at the slices of toast, drink, and meat from the boxes he brought with him and spread out on the blanket.

"Leave them to the birds, they'll thank us," he runs to the other side of the jeep, sitting in the passenger seat. "Do you see the silver button? Press it to start the engine, and these are the clutch, brake, and accelerator pedals," he shows me with his hand, inadvertently touching my legs.

My fingers grip the steering wheel. I should tell him that he's completely wrong about me and I can't drive, or I should I press the silver button? I must decide.

My fingers reach the button, and I press it, hear the engine's vibration as it turns on, and my hand grips the steering wheel even more tightly.

"Now, gently press the clutch pedal," he leans towards me and points, and I lift my leg and press it as gently as I can, and he shifts gears.

"And now release," he whispers to me, and I move my leg, and the jeep immediately shuts off.

"Again, push the silver button," he takes my finger and makes sure I don't regret it. I press the clutch again and rerelease it, this time trying to be gentler, and the jeep starts to drive slowly in the field. I want to scream in fear and joy; I'm driving.

"Great, keep the wheel steady," he leans close to me, giving me directions, but I'm not focused on his body odor and the fact that he's so close, my eyes are fixed on the dirt road we slowly drive on, and my whole body is tense.

"It's too fast. We'll turn over," I whisper to him.

"It's a low gear, the jeep won't overturn. I'll close my eyes, I won't look," he covers his eyes with his visor while the jeep advances slowly down the road.

"Henry, everything's shaking."

"Grace, you're the pilot. I'm the blind co-pilot."

"What direction should I turn?" I yell at him as we approach a blue road sign with the name 'Anzio' written on it.

"It seems to me that we are going to Anzio," he lifts his visor for a moment before returning it and covering his eyes.

"Henry, we'll roll over," I shout at him but want to scream with joy, and despite the slow speed in which I drive, I can feel the wind trying to let my hair come undone. But as we approach the small town, I stop the jeep and don't want to go further.

Many houses, on both sides of the street are ruined, and far away, at the beach, I can see gray wrecks of landing crafts standing in the water, as the waves hit them with white foam. Along the main road, leading to the town, stands several German ruined tanks with their cannons pointed at the sea, as if still threatening the shore, even though the Germans had already been chased away from here.

"Let's go a different way," I say to Henry and get out of the jeep.

"It's not a place for us. Let's go look for a happier place," he says as we change seats. We're passing the Germans tanks, searching for the exit from the town, continuing to drive between houses perforated by bullet holes, and destroyed Americans tanks, but I'm trying not to look at them.

"Stop here," I say and put my hand on his shoulder, hurrying to get out of the jeep once he has stopped.

The flat field on the side of the road is full of white crosses, in straight lines, and I start walking between them, ignoring my leg, even though it's difficult for me to walk on the soft ground.

"Grace, what are you looking for in this place?" He yells at me from the jeep, but I don't answer him. I keep on walking between the white crosses.

"Robert Walker, Robert Walker," I whisper the name again and again, searching line after line, white cross after white cross with my eyes.

"Grace," he shouts again, but I don't answer him. I must find him, know if he's here.

"Robert Walker," it's written on the simple white wooden cross, along with his personal number, and I stand and look at the black letters. Trying to imagine him storming the shore from a landing craft. What did he look like? Was he afraid?

"Did you know him?" Henry asks me, placing a hand on my shoulder, and I shake my head in negation. I didn't even hear Henry as he approached me.

I take John's lighter out of my shirt pocket, look at the engraving 'To Hell and Back' one last time and place it at the foot of the white cross.

"No, I didn't know him, but I pay him final respects," I say to Henry, who's taken off his visor and looks at me.

"Grace, do you have my lighter?"

Without saying a word, I take out his lighter from my pocket, give it back to him; I know I must apologize. I'll apologize to him later.

"Final respects," Henry places his lighter next to Robert Walker's, stands up, and salutes him.

Later, we slowly return to the jeep, pass by the crosses, and read the names.

"You know, Grace," he says, as
we lean against the jeep and look
at the beach and the shipwrecks.
"Sometimes I'm scared to take off
and fly on a new bombing mission,
but really scared," and he takes
the whiskey flask out of his leather
jacket pocket and sips from it, not
stopping.

Only in the evening does he drop
me off at the hospital entrance,
saying goodbye.

"I apologize we didn't manage to
reach Rome," he says. "I wanted to
take a photo with you in front of the
Colosseum."

"At least you taught me how to fly a
little," I smile at him and remember
my hands tightly holding on to the

steering wheel. I know I need to kiss him now, as the other nurses do, but I still can't.

"At least we fed some birds in the field," he smiles at me.

"At least I retrieved your lighter; thank you," I say to him and turn my back, start climbing the stairs to the hospital.

"Goodnight, Grace, you're a good woman," he says to me as he gets back into his jeep.

"And a liar, too," I whisper to myself as I enter the hospital. "At least you didn't discover that I have no leg. Unless Audrey's already told you, and you pity me."

***

"Tell me, Grace, isn't your man back home sending you more letters?" Audrey asks me two days later, as we lay in our beds in the nurses' room at night. She's reading a book, and I'm reading one of Georgia's letters again, the part where she misses riding a bike with John by the river. I already know this paragraph by heart. It always makes me cry.

"No new letters have arrived, but I'm waiting," I stop reading and look at her. Does she suspect something and is testing me?

"And don't you miss him? Don't you write to him?" She asks as she returns to reading her book.

"I write to him," I answer and show her the notebook I have, cover it by my hand, so she won't notice

I didn't tear any pages from it. "I really miss him," I keep saying to her, not telling her how much I miss someone to love; she'll laugh at me.

"Maybe you don't miss him enough," she raises her head from the book.

"What do you mean?"

"I heard Henry took you on a picnic."

"Yeah, he was nice. I didn't want to, but he insisted."

"Yes, he's a kind-hearted man," she replies and returns to her book. "Once, he took me for a picnic in the fields and we saw a bird with a broken wing," she pauses, looking at me. "He wanted to save her, but I said to him that it has no chance and that it'll die anyway."

"Did he save it?"

"I was right," she closes her book and blows on the candle by her bed. "Good night, Gracie."

"He didn't take me to a picnic," I say to her after a few minutes. "He took me to Rome to show me the Colosseum," I fold the letters and put them back in my locker, blowing off my candle, keep talking to her in the dark. "I've enjoyed Rome so much."

***

I place my finger on the jeep's silver starter button and close my eyes, silently saying a prayer. That there's enough gas in the fuel tank for this trip, that no one will stop me on my way out of the hospital, and that I know how to drive well enough to get us to Rome and back.

The engine rattles, and I lift my wooden leg and press the clutch pedal, releasing it gently, feeling the jeep starting a slow and bouncy ride.

"Are you sure you know how to drive?" John asks me and laughs as the jeep rattles again and shuts down in the canter of the front driveway.

"There was a stone here," I reply and start the engine again, trying to concentrate on the pedals and the steering wheel. I need to succeed. I also have to get out of here as fast as I can before someone notices I took a jeep without permission.

One more round of test drive in the

front driveway and one more gear shift training, which is answered with tormented engine noise, and I turn onto the exit, passing the ruined metal gate and the two main cypress trees, starting our journey towards Rome.

The autumn wind makes me quiver, and I'm sorry I didn't bring coats for John and me, but I mustn't think about it now, I have to concentrate on the gear shifting, even though I drive as slowly as I can. It took me such a long time to convince him to join me. I'm too afraid to make this trip myself, and I'm responsible for him, even though he won't be able to help if anything happens to us, but he's the only one I could ask.

After he agreed, I woke him up early in the morning, put his army uniform I had managed to get on the bed.

"Close your eyes," he whispered
to me as he took off his hospital
pajama.

"I'm a nurse. Have you forgotten?"
I didn't mention to him that I'd
already seen his body when he
lay wounded beside me when he
had just arrived, and I thought he
wouldn't live.

"Close your eyes."

"They're closed."

"I don't believe you," he undressed
in front of me, quickly put on the
khaki uniform while I looked at him,
at his chest hair, that was removed
when he was wounded, didn't
grow back yet, and there were
scars all over his chest, which will
darken one day. Still, he looked so
handsome to me, and I was sorry

when he buttoned the shirt of his
khaki uniform.

"Let's go," he took his little
backpack, put on his sunglasses,
reached out his hand, and placed it
on my shoulder.

"Where are you off to so early?"
The nurse on duty asked us. "Grace
wants to show me something,"
he smiled at her, and I touched
his hand, that was placed on my
shoulder, wondering why he was so
good to me.

And now we're driving on the road
heading north, and I'm afraid
of Rome. Afraid I'll fail and that
something will happen.

At the entrance to the village,
near the ruined tank, I slow down

the jeep even more and bypass it gently, smiling at the children sitting on its turret.

"La vedova en moto, la vedova en moto," they yell and wave as soon as they recognize me. "Americana, Pinocchio," they jump out of the tank, and I stop the jeep, smiling at them awkwardly.

"What's going on? Who are they?" John turns to me.

"We're at the entrance to the village," I say to him. "And there's an American destroyed tank thrown by the side of the road that the children like to play on, imagining they're at war. "

"Americana, Americana," they surround the jeep and smile at me and John, who smiles through his sunglasses. How can I explain to him how they know me?

"They love American women. I have no idea why, maybe because of our accent."

"How many are they?" John laughs and extends his hand in their direction, while they laugh at him and hold his hand, theatrically shaking his hand.

"They're five of them, four boys and one girl, and they're lovely." I look at their wild black hair, simple clothes, and big smiles.

John turns to them and spreads his hands wide, as he is a great magician, and they stand in anticipation, occasionally laughing at the sight of his hands and moving fingers.

"Abracadabra," he waves his hands in the air again and then turns to the back of the jeep, groping for his leather backpack, revealing a military chocolate bar from the bag.

"Chocolate," he whispers, while waving the military rationed chocolate in the air, announcing as if he created it out of nothing.

"Bravo," they clap their hands while he opens the package and breaks the chocolate into cubes, fumbling in the air for their outstretched hands. One by one, he gives them the sweet cubes, and they push them into their mouths, chewing and smiling.

"Il circo con il cioccolato," they shout and return to climb the tank.

"Bye, bye, Pinocchio," they wave to

me as I start driving, and I wave back at them. John also raises his hand and waves in the direction of their voices as we slowly enter the village.

"Where's the chocolate from?"

"It was a surprise."

"What kind of a surprise?"

"A surprise I prepared for us for a journey," he says as his head is turned back to the children, even though we cannot see them anymore. "Now it seems to me that the surprise is in their belly."

I want to tell him that he's a good man and that he moved me, but I have to concentrate on driving on the narrow stone streets inside the village, to be careful that my leg does not slip, even though it does every now and then, causing the jeep to jump.

When we arrive at the square, I slow down again and stop, even though it's empty early in the morning and no one is standing by the shattered fountain.

"This is the village square," I describe to John. "In the center stands a white marble fountain and a statue of a proud lion spitting the water to the pool at his feet," I try to imagine what it was like before the war. "Around the square, there are shops and a café, where the men sit for a morning coffee and read the newspaper, soon they'll probably come and greet each other. And at the far end, there is a cinema. Once a week, in the evening, all the men and the women go to see a movie. Now the

movie playing is a romantic one,"
I look at the destroyed billboard in
front of the cinema, covered with
Mussolini posters.

"Thanks," he smiles at me as we
drive out of the village and his hand
a little closer to my thigh, but he's
not touching me.

'To Rome.' A blue sign, attached to
a wooden pole and perforated with
bullet holes, shows us the way, and
I turn the jeep and continue driving
on the dirt road down the hill,
between the cypress avenues.

"Grace, is everything okay?"

What's going on? Something's
wrong with the jeep, it's going down
the hill too fast, what happened
to the breaks? I'm pressing them,

but my legs keep on slipping to the side. What's wrong with my wooden leg?

"Grace, what's going on?" I hear him while my hands hold tightly on to the wheel, trying to stabilize the jeep. Something's wrong with my wooden leg, and the jeep is too fast. My leg slips again and again, no matter how hard I push it against the breaks.

"Grace," he shouts, and it seems to me that he's holding on to me, or trying to protect me, as the jeep keep on driving as if it has a life of its own, continues to turn, and goes down the hill to an olive grove on the side of the road, while I shout and keep pressing the brakes with all my might, holding the steering wheel. I then think something hit me and I scream again.

"Grace, are you okay?" I can feel his hands around me, his warm body leaning on mine. I open my eyes and look around.

We're still inside the jeep, which is lying in a ditch on the side of the road, in an olive grove. My hand slips on my leg, trying to arrange the leather strips through the khaki pants. They've slipped and caused the wooden leg to loosen and change position.

"Grace, are you okay?" I look at him again, his face close to mine, and I examine his eyes, the sunglasses are gone from his face, and I reach out and touch his closed eyes, stroking them gently.

"Yes, I think I'm fine," I reply slowly.

Why did this happen to me? Why did I think I could take us to Rome?

"Can we get out of the jeep? It's safe," he continues to hold me as if guarding me, and I look around.

"Yes, I think we can manage to go out," I stop stroking his eyes. The grove is quiet, and the dirt road is behind us.

John leans back as I carefully get out of the jeep, helping him out, and looking at what I did. Why can't I succeed? Why do I fail in everything I do?

"John, are you okay? I'm going to get help," I say and walk away, limping over to the dirt road and start walking.

"Grace," he's calling after me.

"I'm going to find help," I shout at him and don't turn around.

Go, just keep on going, you mustn't think that you are responsible for what happened. Just keep on walking and look for help. Walk, walk, walk, don't stop walking. It's not you, it's the wooden leg. I limp up the dirt road, and it seems to me that I hear him still calling me, but I can't stop now, I must find help, I'm responsible for what happened, I'm the one who destroyed everything, me, and my leg. I must fix what I did.

I'm ignoring the pain in my leg, my limping, or the sweat covering my body. I'm also ignoring his calls that I almost can't hear anymore. I'll find someone to help me and return things as they were before, when I had a leg; when I had a leg, and when I believed in myself. Another step and another one, I keep going up the hill, I won't give up, I won't stop walking, I must succeed, I'll find a solution.

Just at the top of the hill, I sit down on a rock, raise my khaki pants, remove my wooden leg, rub my sore stump, and start crying.

It's noon when I finally get up from the rock, at the top of the hill, and start going down the path again, slowly limping, looking for John and the jeep, trying to think what to tell him. I'll tell him I went to the village to seek help, and no one was willing to help me. But I know that even he, who can't see, won't believe me. The village is too far away.

The jeep is parked on the side of the road, as if it had never been in a ditch, and John is sitting on the wild weeds next to it. His backpack is open, and he's eating canned meat. I slowly approach, making a deliberate noise and standing in front of him on the wild weeds.

"Are you hungry?" He raises his head at me.

I shake my head, but after a moment I realize that he cannot see me, and I sit down in front of him, reach out my hand and touch his arm. John hands me the canned meat and his fork, and I hungrily eat it. I haven't eaten since the morning.

"I'm sorry," I finally say.

"It's okay."

"I apologize for leaving you alone here."

"I'm blind. I have to learn how to manage by myself," he takes the can of meat from my hand and continues to eat.

"How did you manage?"

"I got help."

But as I continue to ask him, he refuses to tell me more, and we resume eating in silence. I watch his hands groping for the food cans lying in front of him, occasionally raising my eyes to the jeep, standing by the side of the road. How did he manage it alone?

"Thank you for bringing food," I finally say.

"It was the second surprise I

brought with me. I wanted us to sit on the side of the road, on the way to Rome, and eat. The first one was taken by the kids on the tank."

"It's too late. I don't think we'll get to Rome."

"No, we won't get to Rome."

"We need to get back," I say and think that, despite everything I have done, I want to stay and sit with him here under the olive trees, even though I know he's angry with me.

"Can you drive back?" He starts collecting the empty cans, searching for them with his hands.

"Do you trust me to?"

"I'm blind, and we're the only two people here."

I want to keep asking him how the jeep got back onto the road, but I'm ashamed. Maybe soldiers with a truck passed by and helped him, perhaps a tank, connected a cable to the jeep, easily pulling it out of the ditch, but I don't ask again, and he doesn't tell me. Quietly, we collect the empty food cans into his backpack and get into the jeep.

"Start the engine. Everything's okay," John puts his hand on my arm for a second, and I reach for the silver start button and press it, hearing the engine gurgle as the vehicle starts. On a slow ride, while my feet are constantly ready to press the brakes, and the leather straps are tightly attached to my leg, until I have to ignore the pain, I start driving. We return through the village, and I overlook the shattered fountain and the ruined cinema, not stopping near the tank at the entrance to check if the children are still playing.

"Thank you for this day," he finally says as I park the jeep at the hospital's front driveway, behind one of the supply trucks.

"John?"

"Yes?"

"I'm sorry," I say instead of asking how he felt after I abandoned him.

"It's okay," he puts his hand on my shoulder, and we enter the hospital. He goes to his corner and I to my room, waiting for Blanche to call me and punish me for stealing the jeep. Maybe no one noticed.

"Grace," he says before we part.

"Yes? I really do apologize," I approach him.

"Don't give up on Rome," he's walking away from me, groping his way through the hall to his bed, and I don't follow him.

***

"I need a jeep to go to Rome," I stand in her office and watch her. I've been waiting for her to call me to her office since yesterday, and this morning I didn't hold back and went into her room.

"And why do you need a jeep to go to Rome?" She leans back behind her brown wooden table and looks at me.

142

"So I can practice driving," I want to put my hands on the table and explain to her that I must stop being different, but she won't understand me.

"Tell me, Grace, do you belong to the U.S. Army Transportation Corps?" She looks at me with an amused look.

"No, Head Nurse Blanche."

"And are you a girl from a respectable family, say from the Hamptons, with a really rich daddy, who woke up one morning and decided to rebel against daddy and be a racing driver with my jeeps?"

"No, Head Nurse Blanche, I don't have a rich father," I think of my drunken dad and my mom, who work all day, never home. What punishment will I get?

"And do you have any experience driving jeeps, say from North Africa?"

"No, Head Nurse Blanche. I wasn't in North Africa. I arrived from New York to Italy," I say to her, but she already knows that.

"And if I give you a jeep, who will accompany you on your way to Rome?" I look at her and think of the jeep stuck in a ditch and John's arms protecting me.

"I'll find someone," I raise my eyes and look at the gray sea I can see from her window, knowing that there's no one to accompany me on the way to Rome. I abandoned the only person who trusted me. I should've stayed with him.

"So, you can't take a jeep to Rome,

with or without my permission," she once again leans forward and begins to write something on the paper laid on her desk. "And get out of my office. I have a complaint to take care of. Someone took one of my jeeps yesterday."

"Yes, Head Nurse Blanche," I hurry out of her room, closing the door gently behind my back and praying she won't call me again in a few minutes. I won't give up Rome. He also told me not to give up. I have to get boots to cover my wooden leg, that I won't stand out so much.

***

Francesca stops the motorcycle at the side of the road, next to the blue, bullet-riddled road sign, painted with an arrow in the direction of Rome.

"Americana, wait for me here," she leaves me sitting on the running motorcycle and gets off, approaches the sign, lifts the hem of her black dress, kneels at its feet, and pees.

I blush and avert my eyes in the other direction, too shy to look at her, watching the road. I'll warn her should a car come, but no vehicle approaches, and I don't think it bothers her at all.

"Americana let's keep going to that city," she says as she climbs back onto the motorcycle, lifts the hem of her black dress again, and wraps it around her thighs.

"Thank you, la vedova en moto," I

grip her waist tightly and cling to her as the motorcycle continues its bouncy ride on the dirt road. She's the only one who agreed to take me to Rome.

"I don't need your chocolate, Americana," she said to me a few days before, when I approached her as she was sitting in our corner, placing a paper bag full of American Army sweet chocolate bars in her lap.

"Please, take it," I asked her, as she tried to return the bag to me. "I need to get to Rome."

"And that's what you think of me? That some chocolate will make me go to that ugly city?" She tore the bag, and all the yellow packages scattered on the ground between us.

"I have to get there."

"So ask your new friends, who walk around in their fancy white uniforms all day and call me the cursing Italian," she held out her hand, and I gave her a cigarette.

"Please, you're my only friend here. I'm tired of being so different, that everyone's looking at me."

"And how do you think I feel?" She lit the cigarette and looked at me. "La vedova en moto, the widow on the motorcycle. I keep hearing these words wherever I go in my village. Do you think that they won't speak behind your back if you have boots? Americana, you know nothing."

"Please, la vedova en moto, let's go together."

"This city is the devil. Only bad things happened to me when I arrived there."

"But you met your husband there."

"And what did I get out of it?" She blew the cigarette smoke into the sky.

"Please, I have no one else to ask."

"All right, Americana," she looked at me. "We'll go to Rome," her hands collected the chocolate bars from the floor and tucked them into the torn paper bag. "And this is for my child. He deserves a little sweetness in his life."

And now we're driving to Rome on the ruined road, between cypress and olive trees. I'm wearing my khaki army uniform and hugging her waist, and she's in her black dress, as we both ride on her rattling, red motorcycle.

When I recognize the place where the jeep went off the road, into the olive trees, and notice the tire tracks, I look away to the other side, holding her tightly and closing my eyes. How could I leave him alone like that?

"Americana, is everything okay?" She yells at me, trying to overcome the sound of the motorcycle.

"I was in charge of him," I whisper, knowing she won't hear me.

"What?"

"Tell me something about your child. How old is he?" I shout back at her. I'm ashamed to tell her what I did.

"No," she yells back at me.

"Why?"

"Because it brings bad luck, you listen to me, and then you'll leave one day, and it'll bring bad luck."

"Not everything brings bad luck," I hug her tighter, even though I've only had bad luck since I got to this place.

"Believe me, Americana, in this war, everything brings bad luck," she twists the gas handle even harder as we get on a new dirt road with another blue sign pointing to Rome, and I try not to think what people will say when they see us riding on her noisy red motorcycle.

"Viva Italia," a group of soldiers sitting in the back of an army truck shout at us when we bypass them on the dirt road, and I look to the other side so as not to see their smiles. But when we get on the main road and approach the city, the army convoys moving north are endless. One by one, we need to bypass the khaki trucks and the whistling soldiers, and I hug Francesca and close my eyes, letting her lead us through the streets, entering the busy city full of green army trucks and jeeps with the American white star painted on their hoods.

"This is the place where you Americanos take photos," she stops the motorcycle at a large square in front of the Colosseum. I look at all the soldiers standing and holding cameras, taking pictures of their smiling Italian girls.

"Let's take a picture," I say to Francesca as I get off the motorcycle, even though I don't have a camera. I raise my eyes and watch the Colosseum standing above me.

"I'm not taking pictures with you. I thought you wanted to come to Rome to buy boots, not to be like all the Americans, who bring here their new Italian girlfriends they bought with cigarettes and chocolate," she looks around at all the soldiers and their girls walking around us, wearing floral dresses, and laughing.

"Smile," I move away from the motorcycle and act as if I'm photographing her.

"I'm not smiling," she looks at me but smiles a little.

"Now I have a photo of you from Rome," I smile back at her and look around. Everyone around us seemed so happy and cheerful, as if the war was over and there were no more battles against the Germans in the north.

"Will you take a picture of me?" I ask her.

"Smile, Americana, and look at the Colosseum, like all Americanos," she finally raises her hands as she takes a photo of me. Still, when I'm looking aside, I can see a soldier passionately kissing his girl while she hugs him tightly.

"Let's get out of here," I slowly limp back to the motorcycle.

"Americana, don't you want a photo?" She looks at where I looked before.

"No, I've changed my mind," I'm trying to lift my leg and get on her motorcycle, ignoring the stairs around me."

"Americana, she has an ugly dress," she whispers to me as I climb back on the motorcycle, and we continue to ride the city streets. I know she's lying but won't stop hugging her.

"What is this?" I ask her as we pass in front of a vast white building, made of marble columns and sculptures of bronze horses at his fronts.

"It's this city's wedding cake," she replies as she rides between the military trucks and the local men wearing suits and riding bicycles "We once had King Victor Emmanuel, who wanted to be remembered, so he built himself an ugly white wedding cream cake."

"It looks like a typewriter," I yell at her, trying to get over the noise of the motorcycle and the trucks driving around us. But she doesn't reply and steers through the narrow streets, bypassing military jeeps or small armored vehicles, cursing at their drivers. Finally, she stops on a street full of luxury shops, and we both get off the motorcycle, looking around.

It seems like the war had never visited this part of the city, there are no bullet holes in the walls of the buildings and none of the building are destroyed, the cafés are full of soldiers and civilians sitting around small tables, and the air smells of real espresso. Women in fashionable dresses stand by the shop windows. Only the newsboy walks down the street, holding a bunch of papers under his arm, and shouting that the Russian army has occupied Prussia. But it seems to me that no one here is interested in the war around, while he keeps calling out the news loudly, hoping, in vain, that someone puts a coin in his hand and buys a newspaper.

"Let's buy my boots and get out of here," I say to her as we walk down the street, examining the shoe store windows.

"Americana, where's your money?"

"Why?" I place my hand on my backpack, feeling my wallet inside.

"Americana, where's your money?"

"Here, in the backpack," I look around, checking to see if anyone is trying to approach and pickpocket me.

"Where is it? Give it to me."

I take out my wallet and hand her the bills I brought, and she takes most of it and walks away from me.

I start walking after her, watching how she goes to one of the house's entrances, approaching a young woman talking to a soldier standing with his back to us. Francesca starts talking to the soldier in Italian, and it seems to me like she's cursing him while he curses her back in English. Still, she starts yelling and pushing him away from the other woman until he walks away down the street, keeps on cursing Francesca.

The other woman is wearing red lipstick and a black dress, but simpler than Francesca's, and one of her dress shoulder straps is dropped, exposing her white bra.

I begin to approach them, but when she notices me, she starts moving back into the shadows of the house's entrance.

"Americana, wait there," Francesca turns to me, going back to talking to the young woman, placing a hand on her arm for a moment. She wears torn black tights and worn-out high heels.

"Let's get out of here," Francesca comes back to me after giving her something. The woman has disappeared into the dark stairwell as if she'd never existed.

"Where is my money?"

"Let's get out of here. You don't need it."

"It was my money."

"You don't need it. She needs it more than you do. We'll buy you boots elsewhere," she keeps walking towards the motorcycle, and I limp after her, passing the café full of smiling soldiers and Italian girls. They sit next to the boot shop, whose fancy boots are displayed in the window. These were supposed to be my new boots.

"Stay here," Francesca says to me, after a few minutes of

driving through the narrow alleys, between peddlers 'carts and cyclists; she passes in places where vehicles can't enter and parks the motorcycle next to several peddlers' carts.

The small square, surrounded by reddish buildings with peeling plaster from their walls, is full of people standing and talking to the merchants, who spread their wares on blankets in the middle of the street— silverware, shoes, clothes, matches, and cigarettes.

From the side, I see how she approaches one of the merchants and starts arguing with him, pointing to a pair of boots. He answers her, and for a moment, it seems to me that they'll start hitting each other, but finally, they smile and shake hands while he hands her the high boots in exchange for what's left of my money, and she approaches my hiding place, behind one of the peddler's carts.

"Your new boots, Americana," she hands me the second-hand boots, and I feel the smooth brown leather and the buckles, wanting to hug her. Finally, I won't stand out as much.

"Thanks, la vedova en moto."

"Let's get out of here. I hate this city," she climbs on the motorcycle and starts it, and I sniff my new boots for another moment before tugging them into my backpack, climbing on the motorcycle, behind her.

Only when we drive away from the city, towards the exit, and pass the signs pointing the way back to the south and Naples, does she park the motorcycle on the side of the road, next to a ruined building. We both sit on the ground and lean against an old wall, and I take out a lunch box I brought with me.

"I'm afraid of Rome," she says after a while. "This city scares me."

I look at her and say nothing.

"What scares me the most is that I'll become like that woman in the alley," she takes out a cigarette and lights it. "A woman without a husband and with a small child, a woman that's willing to do anything to get some money to buy her child food."

I place my hand on hers, thinking of what to say.

"Don't feel sorry for me,
Americana," she looks at me and
blows the smoke into the sky.
"But for me, it's the scariest thing,
having to be like her."

"You won't be like her."

"This is what is left at the end of
a war, widowed women who're
selling their bodies to soldiers," she
whispers.

"Let's finish eating and go back to
your village. Your child is waiting
for you," I stroke her arm. I wish
someone was waiting for me.

***

13. Henry.

"You don't come to the club anymore," he watches me as he stands next to his jeep, his hand holding a bouquet of bougainvillea. He had probably picked them from the bush near the ruined gate while he stopped for a moment as he was coming over.

"Yes, I had a lot of work to do," I look at him. He has a nice smile. John also has a nice smile, but I don't have the courage to come to his bed at night again.

"Didn't you enjoy our last trip? Did visiting Anzio sadden you?" He comes closer, walks up the stairs and gives me the flowers.

"I really enjoyed that day," I take

the colored branch from him. I don't have to think about John. I am trying not to think about him ever since.

"The birds in the field whispered in my ear that they're grateful for the food we left there. I met them the last time I flew, and they asked me to tell you that in person."

"So that's the reason that you came over, to tell me about the birds?" At least Henry is interested in me, unlike John, who loves a woman back home that no longer loves him.

"Of course that's why I came over, and also to give you a formal invitation."

"What formal invitation?"

"Dear Ms. Grace, the honorable

transport driver in the khaki uniform, will you kindly come and visit me at our glorious club? You don't come anymore," he smiles and bows. I'm still in my khaki pants. I don't have the courage to wear my nurse dress and new boots.

"And if I refuse, will you offer the flowers to some other girl?"

"If you refuse, I'll have to invite you to a picnic again, or maybe I'll take you on a trip to Rome. Have you been to Rome?"

"I've not been to Rome," I look at him, reminded of the soldier who kissed his girl in front of the Colosseum. I shouldn't think about John, he'll never kiss me. I have to believe in Henry.

"Mr. Henry, the honorable bomber pilot, I promise to come," I bow and smile at him, but my fingers play with the flowers I'm holding, scattering them on the white floor of the front steps.

"Bye Gracie, I'm waiting for you," he gets back to his jeep and exits the ruined gate, and I think that only two other people call me Gracie, one of them I hate, and I shouldn't get attached to the second one.

I keep standing and watching the jeep move away until it disappears behind the bend and the cypress trees, leaving a slight cloud of dust and a pungent scent of burnt gasoline at the front driveway.

Does Henry really like me, or am I some funny amusement on his way to the next girl? I need to talk to someone. I also need to apologize to John.

***

He's not in the garden among the other wounded, sitting in white chairs covered in woolen blankets, the white bench overlooking the sea and the sun before sunset is also empty. He's not in his bed either, and Edward, the wounded soldier lying next to him, doesn't know where he went. I ask the on-call nurse where he could be, but she tells me she only saw him taking his cane, hitting it on the floor, and going out of the hall.

Only when I go out to the hospital's front stairs and look around do I see him. He's standing by himself on the ruined road, far away from the hospital. What is he doing there?

I hurry down the stairs and cross the large parking lot, ignoring the

pain in my leg from walking on
the gravel, crossing the iron gate,
getting close to him.

He stands in the middle of the road
and moves from side to side; his
hands are raised as if embracing an
invisible lover while dancing with
her to the sounds of an imaginary
melody.

I try to walk towards him, as quietly
as I can, approaching him slowly
and reaching out my hands to take
his, but a few steps before I can
hold on to him, he stops dancing
and turns to me.

"Hey, Pinocchio, how are you?"

"I came to dance with you," I
approach a few steps further,
touching the palms of his hands.

"I enjoy dancing alone," he releases
his hands from my fingers.

"Would you invite me to dance with you in the autumn sunset?"

"I'd be happy to keep on dancing by myself," he bends down to the road and searches for his cane with his hands, lies down, picks it up, and turns his back to me. He slowly moves away, further down the road, hitting the ruined asphalt with the stick.

"I thought you'd be happy to dance with me," I shout at him from a distance, not approaching anymore. "And I also have new boots; I wanted to tell you."

"So, you told me," he starts dancing with his imaginary loved one again, hugging her in his arms.

"And I also want to dance with you."

"What's changed?" He turns to me.

"Did you come to pity the blind soldier and clear your conscience?"

"No," I cringe. "I wanted to see you."

"No, you didn't come to see me. You wanted to tell me how nice you were recovering and that you have new boots."

"But I also wanted to see you," I feel the leather of the boots tighten on my feet, and I try to move from side to side, standing on the road.

"You wanted to see me before or after you left me there alone, in the ditch, with the jeep?"

"I'm sorry, I thought you were fine," I say, holding my hands together. "When I came back to you, you weren't angry with me."

"You left me alone in the dark, Grace, alone. You abandoned me. I'm blind," he feels his way towards me with his stick but stops at a distance and doesn't get any closer. "Shall I tell you how long it took me to find the jeep after I tried to chase you when you ran away? Shall I tell you how many times I fell in the dark, scratched from the thorns and the rocks as I felt my way back to the jeep?"

"I apologize. I'm so sorry," I look up at him and feel the tears coming down. "I was stressed. It's all my fault. I wanted to find a way to get the jeep out of the ditch," I want to get close to him, but I know I can't, he'll reject me again.

"Why were you stressed? Because you were with a blind man? Is that what you do when you're stressed, run away?"

"I didn't run away. I went to seek help. I wanted to rescue you."

"I don't need you to rescue me, and you didn't rescue me. Someone else rescued me.

"What happened there?"

"What does it matter?"

"Please tell me," I can feel the tears on my cheeks.

"A man, I don't even know who he was, helped me," he lowered his hands. "He and his two donkeys. An Italian man who probably passed by and saw me sitting on a rock and felt sorry for me, because that's how it is, everyone feels sorry for me, you too."

"I don't feel sorry for you," I say to him quietly, but he keeps talking.

"I don't even know what he looked like and how old he was, but from his slow speech, I think he was an old man," he stands close to me and gasps.

"You know," he continues after a moment, "I didn't understand a word of what he said to me, but he approached and kept on talking in Italian, putting a rope in my hand, and together we tied the jeep to his donkeys. He and I, and his two Italian donkeys, pulled the jeep out of the ditch — an old Italian man, who patted me on my shoulder and probably greeted me. I have no idea because I didn't understand a word of what he said before he disappeared into the darkness and left me alone again. Shall I tell you how my hands were scratched when I pulled the ropes with him?" He raises the palms of his hands, and I see the scratch marks on his hands and want to stroke them but remain standing in my place.

"An old Italian man helped me, and now you came to show me your new boots? So, if you didn't notice, I'm blind. I can't see your new boots."

I want to tell him that I wanted to let him feel them, see them with his fingers, but it's too late now. My boots don't matter anymore.

"John, trucks are coming," I yell at him as I hear a noise approaching, turning around and seeing them. The army trucks approaching us beyond the turn are driving fast, and I want to help him move away from the road, but John already hears them and walks to the side while I follow him and stand a few feet away.

One by one, the khaki trucks with the white star on their sides pass us in an endless convoy heading north, and I stand and watch the soldiers sitting inside them. They're wearing steel helmets and holding their weapons, smiling at me as they pass.

"Come and join us, be our mascot," someone yells at me from one of the trucks, and I just smile at him, but after him, there are a few more who whistle and shout at me to come join them in the war, and I stand and watch, smile back at them and wave my hand, not answering and looking at John. He just stands with his sunglasses, away from me on the side of the road, and looks at them until it's impossible to know that he's blind.

"You can join them. You've already recovered, you've heard them, they're looking for a mascot to take care of them," I hear him tell me as the last truck has passed, leaving behind only a cloud of brown dust that slowly sinks onto the road.

"You too have recovered and can go back to who you were before. You dance wonderfully on the road and manage fine on your own," I shout at him and turn around, starting to walk back to the hospital.

"Grace, I'm a teacher. I can never go back to who I was before," I hear him yell at me and stop in my tracks.

"I'm a teacher," he says again, and even though I want to keep walking away from him, I turn back.

He stands on the empty road and looks at me, "Back there, at home,

I'm a teacher, an elementary school teacher."

"I used to go into my class every morning, pat my schoolchildrens' shoulders and watch them, see who was tired because he had to get up early and help at home, and who didn't bring a sandwich, offering my own food, telling them I'm not hungry," He keeps on talking, standing on the road and looking in my direction.

"Grace, I'm a teacher. I listen to children, even if I've only met them once," he continues to look at me. "That time, at the entrance to the village, near the ruined tank, there were five of them. One was a little taller and bigger than the others, holding my hand tightly. And there was one there with dirtier hair, but I heard his laughter, he's a happy kid, and there was the girl there who quickly snatched the chocolate from my hand, walked away and laughed, but then went back to get more," he pauses for a moment before he continues. "I even keep a chocolate bar in my pocket to give you for them, for the next time you go there," he puts his hand into the thin coat that he wears and pulls out the bar of chocolate, throwing it towards me, but it falls on the road, stays there laying between us, stands out in its yellow packaging on the ruined asphalt.

"I didn't know."

"Because that's who I am, I'm a teacher. An elementary school teacher at Cold Spring, New York, and now I'm here in this country and no longer know who I am."

"You're still the same person you were before you came to this place. You told me that, at nights, when we used to talk."

"No one here stays the way they were, even if they try as hard as they can, but it doesn't matter anymore. You have pilots to go meet, I heard the other nurses keep talking about them, and I have to wait for a letter from the woman I love and, in the meantime, keep dancing with myself," he returns to the center of the road and continues his dance moves, ignoring my presence. I walk back a few steps, stand and look at him, trying to guess which song is playing in his head as he dances and step on the chocolate bar thrown on the road.

"Nurse. I was a nurse back home,"
I yell at him. "I was an intern nurse
at Mercy Hospital in Chicago, and
I took care of patients. I'd just
graduated from nursing school, but
I wanted more, I wanted to see New
York, the world, I wanted to see the
war that everyone was talking about
on the news."

"I was in Italy for eight days before
I was injured," I keep shouting
in his direction, seeing him stop
dancing and look at me. "Four days
of which in a hospital tent, helping
perform surgery on wounded
soldiers who kept coming in, one
after the other," I can't stop talking.
"The other nurse fell apart after two
days and was evacuated, and I was
left alone, a new nurse, to work
with the doctor. I have no idea what
happened to him in that attack.

Eight days John, I saw the world and the war I so wanted to see for eight days," I wipe away my tears. "And now I'm not sure what's left of me, after this place."

"You stayed the same as you were before," he slowly approaches me.

"No one will take me back at home, I'd never recover, I have no leg."

"I didn't notice, except for your funny walk."

"I hate my funny walk," I scream at him, turning and walking back away. "You're right, you have to wait for letters from the woman you love, and I have a pilot to meet."

***

It takes me a while to find the corrugated iron hut at the dark airport in the evening. The other girls had already gone there ahead of me, and by the time I entered our bedroom at the hospital, it was already empty. I still managed to see them from the window, giggling and getting into the pilots' jeep, but I didn't want to shout at them to wait for me.

It took me a long timeto put on my white nurse's dress and my new boots, look at myself in the mirror, and take it off, fold it back into my small metal locker and put back on my loyal khaki pants and regular shoes. And it also took me time to sit in the hospital parking lot, in the stolen jeep, wiping off the sweat from my forehead despite the cool breeze and forcing myself to press the small silver start button.

And now I'm sitting in the jeep, outside their club, having driven slowly through the village, making sure not to shift gears, that my wooden leg won't slip again, holding the steering wheel tightly and sigh in relief as I turn off the engine in front of the hut.

Jazz music emanates from the hut club, and I look up to the sky, watching the silhouette of the dark control tower. I need to get in.

My finger touches my lips and feels the thick layer of red lipstick I applied, trying to make them as prominent as I can, hoping that no one will look at my feet. I had to bring the lipstick with me in case I had to fix it, but I couldn't.

For a second, I'm struggling with the urge to stay here and listen to the crickets outside and the music coming from the lit door, or maybe turn around and drive back to John. But what's the point in that? It won't change a thing, he has a woman he misses, and I have a pilot to meet.

Slowly I get out of the jeep and walk on the gravel, towards the open door, that invites me in. This is the right place for me.

At the entrance, I stand for a moment and look inside. There are fewer pilots and girls in the club tonight. The Transportation Corps female drivers have also disappeared, maybe they're bringing more ammunition in endless convoys, feeding the war monster in the north. Only a few pilots stand by the bar, and a few more sit at the small tables, entertaining the nurses, or maybe vice versa. No one's noticed me yet, I still have time to regret and turn back.

"Grace, come and join us," Henry notices me standing at the door and waves at me, invites me to come, and I see him bend over and say something to the other girls, but I can't hear what he's whispering to them.

"Meet my date for the lovely picnic," he announces and gets up from his chair as I approach, bringing me a chair from a nearby table, and I sit with the others, lowering my eyes.

"Do you hear?" Henry raises his voice over the music as he places new glasses of whiskey on the table. "It's for you, special delivery of gin," he puts the glass in front of me. "It's not every day that someone goes out to try and persuade a girl to go with him on a trip to Rome, and in the end, completely fails in his attempt to reach his destination."

"Maybe she just made him linger on the way," one of the other pilots say, making everyone laugh.

"Or maybe you choose different destinations," another girl adds to the sounds of laughter.

"I like the red lipstick you're wearing," Audrey leans over and whispers to me, "That's exactly the color I have."

"Thanks," I smile at her and grab my glass of gin, sipping it in one gulp. I won't tell her where I got it from.

"She told me she wanted to see Anzio," Henry keeps talking loudly.

"A toast to the ground infantry mice that fought in Anzio," another pilot joins us, stands behind me, and I hear his loud voice as he picks up his glass of whiskey.

"I'd rather be an infantry mouse," laughs one of the pilots sitting at the table with us. "At least if I'm injured, such a beautiful nurse will take care of me," he puts his head on one of the nurses' shoulders while everyone laughs.

"He's right," Henry declares, raising his voice again. "If the German Krauts hit our plane, what will happen to us?" He pauses for a moment and looks around. "If we were lucky and managed to get out of the burning plane, and if the poor parachute has opened, and if we were lucky enough to reach the ground alive, where will we land? On German soil, and who will take care of us? Ugly Inge from Berlin, what kind of justice is that? Friends," he stands up and keeps talking. "I want to be an infantry mouse, too."

"Just like that," one of the girls answers him, and everyone laughs. "We want to treat you, if you're injured, not some Kraut Nazi pilots."

"The right place for German pilots is in a cemetery, not under the caressing hands of beautiful nurses like you," another pilot replies, and the sounds of laughter increase while the girls are looking at me and laughing. I reach for one of the full glasses on the table and drink it too, sipping the burning drink. I don't care who's it is.

"So why didn't you reach Rome?" Audrey asks and leans over Henry. "Did the lady detain you?" She looks at me, and I lower my eyes, searching for another drink for me.

"The lady didn't detain me," Henry touches the pilot's wings attached to his uniforms with his finger. "The lady wanted to learn how to fly."

"I want to learn how to fly too. Why don't you teach me?" Another nurse leans against his other shoulder.

"Girls, this is just a legend," another pilot laughs. "Our jeeps are meant for operational missions only. They're not meant for travel to Rome and certainly not for amusement."

"True, you're just having fun inside your bomber planes. That's the reason they were designed so big, you don't really care about the bombs you are carrying," one of the nurses replies, snatches his hat from his head, wears it, and salutes him.

"Miss," he salutes her back. "We're just fighting in our planes, I swear," he puts his hand on his chest to the sound of the audience laughing, and I look up and see that more pilots have joined and stood around our table, holding glasses of drink and laughing. I must get up and walk away. I'll never be one of them.

"And now, let's dance in honor of Anzio's ground infantry mice," says someone, and the pilots reach out to the women, inviting them to dance. I see Henry asking Audrey, and she willingly rises from her chair.

"Can I invite you to dance?"
Someone is asking me.

"She doesn't like to dance," Henry
tells him, and the pilot pulls his
hand back, looking around, but I
get up from the table and smile
at him, hold his hand and lead us
to the small dancefloor, which is
already filled with pilots and other
nurses wearing white uniforms. I'm
tired of sitting alone in the company
of empty whiskey glasses and
cigarette smoke.

Gently, his hands are holding
my waist, and I'm getting closer,
smelling his clean uniform and
looking at the medals on his chest.
He has a pleasant scent, and he
holds me tightly as we dance while I
try to follow his lead.

I missed dancing so much, and I
don't care about my pain, it'll wait

until the end of the evening. For now, all I care about is the soft music and the muscular hands holding me. I don't even remember his name, even though he told it to me a moment ago, when he introduced himself. It seems to me that my body is trying to remember movements I'd forgot, and I hope he doesn't notice my limp, but I know he does, even though he's polite and says nothing. I close my eyes and place my head on his chest, smelling the scent of his cologne. He surely noticed my limp, everyone did.

"Can I dance with your girl?" I open my eyes and see Henry standing next to us, holding his hand.

"I thought you had another girl," he replies, and I look aside to see Audrey leaning against the bar, sipping a drink, and looking at us.

"Please. One dance, then I'll give her back to you, I promise," Henry smiles at him. "She promised me a dance back then, on the trip to Rome that ended in Anzio, and did not keep her promise."

"The lady is all yours," the pilot smiles at me goodbye before walking to Audrey, asking her to dance, and I smile back at him, letting Henry hold my hand, but make sure to put some distance between us.

"I thought you didn't like to dance," he whispers to me, trying to bring us closer.

"I thought I didn't promise you a dance on our trip," I keep my distance from him.

"I was thinking of a reason to put you back in my arms."

"You thought of a bad one. I've never been in your arms, and I think there are other girls who enjoy being in your arms."

"I think you enjoy being in someone else's arms too."

"Yes, I enjoyed it," I stand in the center of the dance floor, between the other dancing couples. "He was nice, and he didn't make fun of me and our trip together. I'm sorry, I had a long day, and I'm nauseous," I turn to leave the club. Maybe after I go, they'll be able to continue telling jokes about the intern nurse he tried to take to Rome or about the time they let her take care of the German pilot, hoping she'd kill him by mistake.

"Grace," I hear him calling, but I don't stop and walk out of the club, feeling the cool breeze blow in my face as I get out to the silence of the night.

"Grace, I'm sorry, I'll take you back," he walks after me.

"Thanks, but I'm fine," I keep walking slowly, careful not to stumble on the gravel. My leg is in pain, I shouldn't have danced.

"But how will you get back?"

"Did you forget that you taught me to drive? Did you forget why we didn't get to Rome, and you didn't get that photo you probably wanted, another souvenir of you kissing a nurse in front of the Colosseum?" I say and keep walking.

"Grace, I'm sorry for what happened inside," he approaches me. "The trip with you was special to me, but I didn't want to say it in front of the others," he stands close to me as I lean on the jeep, and I smell his leather jacket mixed with the smell of cigarettes. I so want to believe him but I know he's lying.

"Sorry, but I have my own carriage to take me to my castle," I smile at him. He means no harm. This is the man he is, wandering between women. He said it from the beginning, and I knew exactly who he was. I'm just a comic relief for him, to pass the boring time between the other nurses.

"Please, give me just one moment. Don't run away, please," he touches my arm for a second and disappears into the club, and even though I didn't reply, I keep on standing and looking at the open door of the hut.

He's probably promising Audrey a trip to Rome in the near future. I lean against the hood of the jeep and hug myself. The last few nights have become cold. How long do I have to wait for him?

"Problem solved," Henry gets out of the club and holds my hand. "Your jeep will return to the hospital safe and sound. One of the pilots will return it. Now, will you please let me apologize for my behavior and drive you back?"

I don't answer but let him hold my hand, and we walk to his jeep, hand in hand, start driving in silence on the dirt roads of the airport. I run my fingers over my lips, feeling what's left of the lipstick covering them. I shouldn't have taken Audrey's lipstick. I need to get my own red one.

The big bombers flicker in the jeep lights before disappearing in the dark as we pass them, but this time I'm not counting them, I just keep thinking about my lips.

Henry says nothing but also doesn't put his hand on my thigh or try to touch me. He's just focused on driving, like counting the planes. If he tries, I'll let him put his hand on me. I'm so pathetic.

"Please come with me," he says as we stop the jeep near one of the planes, and I can already recognize Betty with her red swimsuit painted on the bombers' nose, lying in her seductive position, with her flowing hair drawn on the silver fuselage.

Only the sound of our footsteps is heard on the gravel as I follow him towards the plane, and I know I need to turn around and get back in the jeep. Maybe it's better to sit alone at the table and watch everyone else dance.

"Feel it," he gets close to me and takes my hand, brings it to the metal fuselage of the plane, and I feel his warm fingers, and once again smell the scent of the pilot jacket he's wearing, as our fingers slide on the cold, smooth metal until I feel a hole and sharp torn steel.

"What is it?" I release my hand from his grip and turn to him, leaning back on the plane and feeling the sharp metal scratching my back.

Henry takes a lighter from his jacket pocket and lights it, brings it closer to the plane's fuselage, and I see that the whole side of the plane is full of holes and torn metal pieces.

"Bullets from a German plane," he says quietly and turns the lighter off as we keep standing, facing each other in the dark. "Over Munich, from yesterday. But we managed to return. Tomorrow or the next day, they'll fix the holes, and we'll set out on a new mission."

I stroke his jacket and reach for the pocket, take out the lighter and turn it on, look at the shell holes again, touch them with my fingers, examine the torn metal. I then give it back to him, enough, I've already taken one lighter from him.

"You can take that one too," he smiles at me in the dark, "So you have a souvenir from me if something goes wrong."

"Keep it with you," I don't want to take a souvenir from him, and I don't want anything to go wrong, but the palm of his hand closes my fingers on the lighter, refusing to take it back.

"You know," he says after a while "Even though we fly at high altitude, and it's cold outside, sometimes it's so hot inside the plane, and I feel the sweat dripping inside the overall I'm wearing, feel suffocated by the parachute and the yellow lifejacket tied around my body. And all around me is the noise of the engines that I pray won't stop working, or that the Germans won't hit them, and that they'll keep working until I land safely. And there's the radio going off in my ear, that I hope won't become the screams of a wounded gunner from my plane or that a plane flying next to me won't become a ball of fire. And the sky around us is full of black clouds of anti-aircraft shells waiting for us to go inside, to our destination, and I can't escape, I must fly straight to the black hell of German planes and anti-aircraft canons that are waiting for us," Henry keeps talking, and I feel his hand holding my arm as if looking for some support. I search for his jacket pocket, pull out the whiskey flask, and serve it to him.

"Most of all, I'm afraid of the pre-flight briefing," he sips his drink and serves it to me, and I make myself drink; I don't want him to feel alone "When the intelligence officer stands inside the briefing hut, in front of his maps and aerial photos, explaining the target we need to bomb to us," he sips again and keep talking "He points to the big map hanging on the wall, reviews the anti-aircraft canons and the German fighter squadrons waiting for us, looking to blow our planes up to balls of fire. In order to get the plane down, they always aim at the engines or the nose, to hit the pilots," he sips again. "You know, Grace," I think he's trying to smile at me in the dark of the plane "I've been in this business for two and a half years. I started in England, and I bombed in Germany, and I continued in North Africa, and I bombed in Germany again, and now I'm in Italy, and I still take off every other day to bomb over Germany," I touch his jacket, look up and reach out my hand, stroking the back of his neck.

"Thirty-four bombing missions so far," he pauses, and I'm not sure if he's shivering for a moment or if it's the cold of the night "My plane was hit Five times, two of my machine gunners were killed by anti-aircraft fire, and once my co-pilot was seriously injured by bullets from a German fighter," I stroke his cheek "That's a pretty fair total relative to the number of missions I did, isn't it?" He picks up the bottle, sips from it again, and gives it to me, but it's empty when I put it to my lips.

I lift my head and start kissing him, my hand gripping the back of his neck, stroking his short hair. He has pleasant lips, and despite the smell of whiskey and cigarettes that remains between us, I can still smell the cologne from his neck. I'm glad I'm also wearing some cologne.
At first, he hesitates, but then, his hands tightly wrap around my body, and he leans on me, and I feel

the cold plane's metal in my back and through my uniform. I keep on kissing him as hard as I can, ignoring the scratches of the torn metal on my back. I need to keep kissing him. He deserves the touch of my lips, and maybe they'll banish his fears. I don't care now if he tells this story to every girl he brings here, to his Betty. Still, I so want to believe that I'm special.

"Thank you for listening to me," he says to me later, as we sit in the jeep at the hospital entrance', "If I were injured, I'd like you to take care of me."

"Thanks," I reply, hoping that he'll never come to this place as a wounded soldier.

"I'll be happy to meet you again, to show you my plane," he strokes my arm.

"Me too," I reply to him as I get out of the jeep, stand on the front steps and watch him as he drives, my eyes following the lights of his jeep moving away until they disappear behind the bend.

Despite the late hour, I couldn't sleep; he kissed me. Will he want us to do more than that the next time we meet? What will I do then?

***

I can't sleep, and I walk to the back of the building, stepping into the dark and empty garden. The white deckchairs stand on the grass waiting for the wounded soldiers to sit on them tomorrow, and I pass through them and sit on the bench that overlooks the sea, letting my hair down after it's been up all evening.

What will he want us to do the next time we meet? Will he want us to do what the other girls giggle about as they whisper to each other in our room at night?

The cool night wind blows the hair onto my face, and I have to pick it up again, even though I want to leave it as it is. I searched for someone who'd like to be with me for so long, but now, I feel my stomach aches.

"He likes me," I turn around and whisper to the few windows of the building that are still lit, watching the faint yellow light emanating from Blanche's room. "And I like him," I add, taking a few hairpins out of my pocket, tightening my hair back to its place.

My fingers loosen the leather straps holding the prosthetic leg, and I am scratching my stump, massaging it and trying not to hurt myself. Why would he want a damaged women like me?

"He's not making fun of me behind my back. He told me I was special," I say to the bench and clean what's left of the lipstick I applied at the beginning of the evening with my fingers, rubbing hard and also wiping the taste of his lips.

"And he wants to be with me. That's all that matters," I light a cigarette and ignore the taste of the smoke that makes me nauseous.

"He'll be my first," I talk to the bench and take the scissors out of my military coat pocket, open them and hold the scissor's blade tightly with my hand.

I carefully start engraving on the bench, to the light of the lighter I'm holding with my other hand. My hand grips the scissors' blade as I try to hurt the wood as much as I can, creating in it a drawing of Henry's bomber with its propellers and wings. At least he wants me, even though I'm crippled.

"I have to accept what others are willing to give me," I whisper, again and again, making another scrape and another scrape in the hardwood of the bench; I must be able to hide my damaged leg. No one else will want me. I don't have to think about John, he doesn't think about me either.

My fingers pull sharp pieces of wood from the scraped bench as I continue to engrave his plane, cutting the cockpit and the black machineguns jutting out in every direction.

"It must be at night, in the dark," my fingers close the lighter, turning the flame off. I look around at the darkness with only the moon and the stars above, trying to spot the lounge chairs on the grass, I then look at the sea, trying to see the foam of the waves. What about my wooden leg? Can I see it in such darkness? What about inside his closed jeep or inside the dark plane? It must be really dark. I'll keep his lighter so that he doesn't make even a tiny light.

"The boots, I'll wear my boots," I bend down and fasten the leather straps to my amputated leg, forcibly tightening them and checking through the khaki pants with my fingers. Without the boots, I can feel the straps and the leg. I'll check again while wearing the boots. When he touches me, he mustn't think that something's wrong.

I won't let him touch my leg. I'm holding the scissors' blade on my thighs, feeling the sharp metal hurt the skin and create a stripe of pain. He mustn't touch me under this line.

"He always brings me back in his jeep. He likes me," I inhale the smoke one last time before I put out the cigarette and toss the butt to the ground. I'll kiss him a lot, so he thinks about my lips.

When the other girls in the room talk about the pilots and laugh with one another, they always whisper about spreading their legs, I'll spread my legs as wide as I can.

I lie back on the bench and try to spread my legs. How will it feel when he lies on me like that? Will his body be heavy for me? Will I like the feeling like the other girls who whisper about it at night? But the most important thing is that I like him and that he wants to do it with me.

***

The other girls in the room are already asleep when I enter, and I undress in the dark. They must've come back when I was with Henry by his plane or when I was sitting on the bench, facing the sea. My fingers search for my locker, and I place my clothes in it, loosen the prosthetic leg's leather straps, quietly placing it on the floor.

"Tell me, Grace, did you use my lipstick?" I hear Audrey whisper to me, but I don't answer her.

"Did you think it would make him fall in love with you?" She continues without waiting for me to reply. "You're so naive."

I lie down on my bed and cover myself with my military wool blanket, trying to be as quiet as possible.

"They always take new girls like you to show them the planes at night," she continues. "Letting them feel the smooth fuselage, saying something about the girl painted on the nose in a swimsuit or revealing dress, confessing about longing for the women they left behind, back home, when they went out to fight for our nation."

My fingers massage my amputated leg, pressing it firmly.

"Then they tell you how magical it is to fly," I keep hearing her. "How wonderful it is to be in the sky, like a bird, to see everything so small, and how brave them pilots are, defeating the Germans, showing you the drawing marks of the bombs painted on the side of the plane, proud of themselves for destroying Berlin and Munich," I keep looking at the black ceiling in the dark.

"Then you let them kiss you," her words continue. "You'll be his great prize. Sure, he'll never stay with you, don't worry, you're neither the first nor the last one, surely a new nurse will arrive soon and take your place," my fingers wrap around the rough military wool blanket, gripping it tightly.

"If you're good enough," I hear her slightly laugh. "He'll even draw you on his plane, writing your name on the nose, replacing the previous one, so he can remember his conquest before the next one in line will replace you," I don't move, I want her to think I fell asleep, still, I'm wiping the tears from my cheeks with my hand.

"But at least you'll be like the rest of us, just the way you always wanted to be," it seems to me she's smiling as she whispers, and I scratch my thighs with my fingernails.

Finally, she pauses, and I turn to the wall, trying to peel off pieces of plaster.

"Don't worry," she says after a while. "I didn't tell him you don't have a leg. I wanted to let him find out for himself."

***

"Americana, this is not your church; it brings bad luck," she replies when I ask her to take me to pray. I'm ashamed to tell her that I hardly went to church back home. I don't want her to think I don't believe. I so need to believe in something.

"La vedova en moto," I shout as I follow her to our corner, behind the old shed. "Do you have another place where I can pray?"

"Go to the sea to pray to the lord of the waves," she turns around and answers me, reaching her hand out, asking for a cigarette.

"I can't," I protect the match's flame from the wind with my hands while she lights her cigarette. I can't pray in the sea after I threw away the cross that was on my neck. He must be waiting for me for revenge.

"You're Americana, you can do anything," she exhales the smoke and stomps her feet. For several days now, the rain hadn't stopped, and we cannot sit on the muddy ground, just stand close to the old shed wall and hide from the rain under the protruding roof.

"Okay, Americana," she says after a while, throws the cigarette into the mud. "Let's go."

"I knew it would be bad luck to take you to church," she yells at me as I hold her waist tightly and try to ignore the pouring rain falling on us, as we ride on the rattling motorcycle.

Her black hair is glistening from the rain and blends with her sodden black dress, which clings to her skin, dripping water on the road, and I have to hold her with all my might as not to slip, feeling the rain penetrating through my military uniform, also getting me wet.

The motorcycle drives slowly through the village paved streets, and I'm afraid we'll slip and turn over at any moment. Maybe I was wrong when I asked her to take me to pray.

"Come on, Americana," she yells at me as she parks the motorcycle on the side of the square and starts running to the church entrance, trying to avoid the rain. But I can't run after her. I have to carefully walk on the smooth pavement and use the stick she once gave me. At least the square is empty, and no one can see how miserable I look; one wet woman walking alone in the dripping rain, crossing the abandoned square.

"Come on, Americana," she shouts at me and goes down the stairs to the rain again, accompanying my slow steps and trying to protect my head with her raised hands, even though the rain is dripping between her fingers and gets both of us wet.

"Come here," she holds my hand as we reach the top step and pulls me inside the church, crossing the heavy brown wooden door.

It takes some time for my eyes to get used to the darkness inside. Still, in the center of the nave, I notice a bright light going down from the roof, down with the dropping rain to the floor, falling on the ruined, wet wood pews that are scattered on the floor, and when I raise my head, I notice a big hole in the church's roof.

"Another gift from some bomber," Francesca says as she notices where I'm looking at and walks inside, bypassing the broken pews towards the apse, looking up at Saint Mary and Jesus and crossing herself, and I do as she does.

Then she goes to one of the rows of unharmed pews, sits, and starts praying in a whisper, and I also sit on one of the wooden pews, but in another row, not wanting her to hear my prayer.

"What shall I do?" I whisper and look up at the saint? "Shall I do with him everything the other girls are laughing about at night?" I try to peek at Francesca, it's just the two of us in the abandoned church. I have to concentrate on my prayer.

"At least there's someone who wants me. Shouldn't that be enough? Even though I didn't tell him that I'm disabled. He mustn't know," my hands are crossed as I keep on praying. "I couldn't tell him. He thinks I was just injured. Is it a terrible sin to lie like that when no one else wants me without a leg?

Why do I keep thinking about John, who loves another woman? Is it awful that I'm lying to him, too?"

But Saint Mary doesn't answer me, and only the rain continues to make a noise, falling from the hole in the roof and hitting the stone floor and the wood fragments lying in the center of the church.

My eyes follow Francesca as she approaches the apse again, holding a candle, lighting it, and crossing herself. I follow her, holding a candle and quietly light it.

"Americana, that's not how you light candles," her cold and wet fingers hold mine as she instructs me on how to place the candle among all the others, and I take another candle and light it, followed by another one and another one.

"Americana, why are you lighting so many candles? Do you think we have a candle factory here?" She whispers to me, but I just look up at Saint Mary, who's watching me from above, and whisper another prayer. For Henry, please make him not be afraid of flying over Germany, asking her to protect him from the German bullets, and for Francesca's husband, asking her to bring him back alive from the cold Russian winter. I also ask her to make John forgive me after I hurt him so much and I don't know how to fix it; and for me, that I'll find someone who'll love me, even though I have no leg.

After I finish and cross myself one last time, I follow Francesca, who's waiting for me at the door, leading me to the corner of the church, to the curved stairs going up to the bell tower, and we both sit on them, waiting for the rain to stop.

"Long before you arrived," she says after a while. "There was another woman like me here, in the village," I watch her fingers arrange her wet dress, trying to separate the black cloth that sticks to her thighs.

"Her husband was drafted into the army, like my husband. Together, they went to Russia," she pauses for a moment. "Then we heard that the Russians had won at Stalingrad and that the Germans and Italians had frozen to death in the Russian winter. The fascist newspapers from Rome said we won, but one person in the village was listening to the BBC, and he told us the truth. And the letters had also stopped coming," she combs her wet hair with her fingers, arranging it.

"I'd see her a lot in the post office when I'd go to the old clerk every day, asking him if a letter had arrived from my husband," she wipes the raindrops from her cheeks. "Or I'd see her here," she gestures at the church with her head. "When I'd come to pray. There was still no bomb hole in the church's roof at that time. And one day, I think after about a year, she stopped praying and started dating a German officer."

I listen to the rain fall and lean against the stone wall, saying nothing, watching her fingers play with the wet fabric of her dress.

"I think she needed to feed her child and had no more money left," she continues. "And she went and prayed to Saint Mary and asked her what to do. She had to choose between standing in the alley in Rome and the gray uniform of the German."

"And what happened to her?"

"I stopped talking to her. Everyone stopped talking to her. Everyone hated her, me too. I would go to the post office and beg the clerk to look at the mailbag again. Maybe he didn't notice, and a letter had arrived, and would see her getting out of her German officer's military car, dressed in beautiful clothes, wearing white leather gloves."

"And is she still here?"

"No," Francesca looks at me. "She disappeared when you arrived.

First, the Germans stopped walking around the village in their clean uniforms, and only soldiers' trucks would cross the main street, on the way south to Naples, carrying German soldiers holding their rifles and staring at us in hatred. And then, before they were really gone and left their mine presents, one day she disappeared. She must've feared revenge. Maybe her German officer took her with him to Berlin. Let's go. We can get back on the motorcycle. I think the rain has stopped."

"Maybe she didn't understand what Saint Mary was telling her," I say to Francesca and get up from the cold stone stairs.

"Maybe, I don't know anymore," she stands up and again arranges the fabric of her dress that clings to her thighs. "I chose to wear a black dress, she chose the Germans," she smiles at me. "She probably didn't think she was worth much."

***

The boots are tightly fastened to my feet. Earlier, when I got dressed, sitting on my simple bed in the nurses' room, I tied the laces as tight as I could, so he couldn't take them off if he tries to, when we'd be together. I'm also wearing a bigger sized dress, so it'll be easier to roll it up.

I take out the lipstick and try to wear it again in the dark, that my lips will stand out as much as possible, even though it's not the red lipstick I wanted. Earlier in the evening, as I was getting ready to go to the club, I looked for the red lipstick in Audrey's locker, but it was gone. I eventually managed to find my old pink lipstick tucked in the bottom of my army duffel bag. I'll have to settle for it.

I lean back in the jeep's seat and look at the darkness outside the pilots' club. He accompanied me to the jeep and asked me to wait for him for a minute, returning to the hut and the music emerging outside, into the night, through the open door. For a moment, I think of the woman in the alley in Rome, and I feel of nauseous, but maybe it's because I drank too much. I'm ready for what we're going to do. That's what I want. And he wants me. I'll never find anyone better than him.

"Sorry for the delay," Henry returns to the jeep and smiles at me, and I smile back, holding the jeep's metal frame tightly. All evening he laughed and smiled and was nice to everyone, and when I got up to go, he volunteered to drive me back.

"No thanks, I'll manage on my own," I replied, knowing he'd insist.

"Let me be a gentleman," he laughed, and some girls laughed along with him while I agreed for him to take me. But Audrey wasn't among them. Tonight, she didn't come at all.

"Shall we go?" He sits in the driver's seat and looks at me.

And I turn to him and smile, saying nothing but feel my stomach cramps

as the jeep begins to drive fast
on the dirt road. At least the rain
stopped, and it isn't as cold outside.

His plane is waiting for us in the
dark while Henry parks the jeep
in front of it, shuts off the engine,
walks over to my side, and gives me
his hand, without saying a word. We
both know why he brought me here.

"Do you have a cigarette?" I ask
him next to Betty's nose, trying
to buy some time, even though I
have my own. Henry hands me the
box and protects the flame with his
hands as I lit myself one, and for a
moment, his face is lit by the yellow
light. He has a pleasant face; he'll
be gentle with me.

We smoke in silence, and I run
my hand over Betty's fuselage,
feeling its smoothness. The torn

metal holes that he'd shown me the previous time had disappeared and had been replaced with shiny new boards. It's nice to stand outside like that, in the cold air.

"That's where we get into the plane," he pulls a handle on the side of the plane, opens a door in the metal body, and I toss the cigarette to the ground and slide my hand on Betty's fuselage and her red painted swimsuit one last time, which looks almost black in the dark.

"Be careful," he is touching my hair as I'm placing my feet on the small metal ladder and climb, bend, and enter the plane. The small space is filled with crates, seats, hydraulic pipes and handles, and I'm carefully feeling around me, trying to see in the dark, noticing the black machineguns.

"This is our real home," he climbs after me, and I can feel his presence close to mine. I'm ready.

"Grace," he's bending over next to me, showing me where to sit with his hand, and handing me his whiskey flask while I lean back against the side of the plane and feel the iron pipes through my dress.

"No thanks," I return the flask to him, feeling his body next to mine on the cold metal floor. I'd already drunk a lot when we were at the club.

"Grace," he tells me again after drinking by himself. "You're different from the other girls, I don't know why."

"It's okay," I answer. I don't want

him to keep talking about how different I am.

"No, it's not okay," he says, and it seems to me that he also had too much to drink. "Just so you'd know, there is a Betty. The real Betty exists."

"We're war wanderers, aren't we?" I feel his body heat through his uniform as we both sit close together, in the narrow space behind the cockpit and the pilots' seats.

"Yes, we're war wanderers," he sips from his whisky again and places his hand on my knee, and I tremble for a moment. Did he feel the leather straps of the prosthetic leg?

"There's only here and now," I place my hand on his fingers, holding them tightly, preventing him from stroking further down to my feet.

"Is everything alright?"

"Yes, everything is fine," I look at his dark silhouette and I can see the moon through the pilots' canopy above us. I'm just like all the other girls.

"You're not like everyone else. I didn't tell anyone about her," he says while stroking my thighs, just as he stroked all those who sat here before me.

"Thanks," I reply, even though I don't believe his nice words.

"I know we're at war and that I may die tomorrow, and that for us there is only here and now, but it was important for me that you know that there is a Betty for me, one

Betty," he drinks again, and I can smell the whisky.

"And what are you to her?" I ask and feel his hand stop stroking my thigh.

"To her I'm just a spoiled and arrogant young man with a sports car and rich parents," he sips from his little bottle again.

"You must be wrong," I whisper to him.

"No, I'm not mistaken," he reaches out and strokes the black machinegun next to him. "That's what I am to her."

"Is that what she told you?"

"She didn't have to," in the dim light of the moon, I can see his hand playing with the bullets belt that is swallowed up in the black machinegun, hearing the rustle of metal under his fingers. "Back home, we always had a lot of money, and a big house, and cars, and I'd go out to parties and hang out. But most of all, I wanted to go with her. She said I was making her laugh."

I try to think what to say but can't, and I put my hand on his thigh.

"But her parents, and my parents as well," he continues. "Always said that nothing would come out of me. Until finally, she refused to go out with me anymore, saying that for in order to get married, one needs a person who takes life seriously."

"And what happened then? Did you try to change?"

"Nothing happened. I kept going out and hanging out and laughing with girls that I can't even remember their names, because that's who I am, a spoiled and arrogant young man that will never take life seriously; even she told me that. And people don't really change," he puts his hand on my thigh again, and I touch his warm fingers.

"After that, Pearl Harbor happened," he sips again. "And I was sitting in the living room of our house and heard the announcer on the radio. I think he was crying. The next day, I ran away from home and went to war," he offers me the whisky again, and I sip from it as he continues to talk slowly. "My dad had a big black Cadillac, he always made sure it was clean and tidy, and he never let me drive it. He once told me that I have to earn the right to drive this car and that I probably never will," I hold his hand tightly, caressing him.

"That day, I took his black Cadillac without asking his permission," he continues. "And drove to one of the Long Island train stations and left it out there in the parking lot, without saying goodbye or even telling him I was going to war. It wasn't even the closest train station to our house," he laughs to himself as he drinks from his whiskey.

"You know, Grace," he strokes my hand in return. "I went to the army, and learned how to fly, and became a captain of a B-17 bomber, but I still drink and smoke and go out with girls I don't remember their names, telling them that war is one big adventure. So, what does that say about me? Does that mean I changed? Or did I stay the same spoiled and arrogant young man?" He sips again.

"I didn't know you then," I stroke his neck, wanting to hug him.

"Deep in my heart," he continues to caress my hand. "I want to hope that the day I get back home, my dad's black Cadillac will still be waiting for me at the train station, right where I left it three years ago, and I'll go in and drive home, and my dad will shake my hand, telling me I've changed. "

I keep stroking his warm hand.

"And I hope," he places his hand again on the black machinegun at his side. "That maybe Betty will wait for me and see that I've changed. But I know it won't happen, people don't change."

I want to tell him that people do change and that he's not the same arrogant young man who got on the train at Long Island station three years ago, but maybe he's right. Maybe people don't change.

I look at his fingers, gently caressing the machineguns' bullet belts, - awaiting tomorrow, for the German planes that would come from the sky - and wonder how many women he did bring here before me, huddle with him in the dark, inside the plane, between boxes of ammunition and machineguns? How many women did look at the black sky through the plexiglass canopy of the cockpit as he told them this story and made them want to fly to the stars with him?

But isn't that the reason I'm here? At least I'm not different from them.

"Will you ever teach me to fly?" I force myself to say. I must do it. He's the only one who wants me.

In the dark, I can notice his smile as he hands me the whiskey again, and I sip from it, emptying what was left, and reach out my hand, shoving the silver bottle in his leather jacket pocket, my hands shaking.

"You're different than everyone else."

"I'm not different," I grab his pilot's jacket and bring my lips closer to his, smelling the whiskey.

"Come with me," he doesn't kiss me back, and to my surprise, he opens the door of the plane, and I feel the cool night breeze penetrating inside.

"Don't be afraid, stand up in the Jeep," he helps me climb into the jeep, "And now, spread your hands as wide as you can," he puts his hand on my back for a moment as I stand in the open jeep, leaning against the windshield and trying to stabilize myself.

"My arms are spread," I shout at him.

"Now, close your eyes."

"I'm scared," I feel the cool night breeze blowing in my face.

"Trust me."

"They're closed," I say to him, even though I keep them open.

"Now lean forward, so you don't fall backwards," he shouts at me and starts driving with the jeep on the dirt runway, increasing his speed. I feel the cold wind hitting my face and ruffling my hair, and only the jeep headlights flicker on the white dirt as he increasingly speeds up, and I look up at the sky and see the stars.

"I'm flying," I shout at him, holding my hands against the cold wind, fighting her back, and not giving up. I want to tell him that he did change and should go back to his Betty, but I'm too embarrassed. I also have to tell my feelings to another soldier, even though he has a woman he thinks is waiting for him back home.

***

"Dear John, even though I didn't receive a letter from you, I know that you'll write to me as soon as you can," I quietly read the words to myself as I lie in my bed. What would Georgia have written to him if she still loved him?

My notebook is laying on the bed, lit by the dim light of the candle. All the other girls in the room are already sleeping, and I must be quiet. I even left my book standing open to hide the small light from the others. If anyone asks what I'm doing, I'll tell them I'm writing a letter home.

As I write down the words, I occasionally put down my pen and look at Georgia's old letters, the ones I keep in my small locker by the bed. Now they're spread out in front of me on the bed while

I'm trying to mimic her rounded and perfect handwriting, though it doesn't really matter. He can't see anyway.

'I keep reading the news that comes from the front every day, trying to guess where you're fighting. All the newspapers are writing about the liberation of Paris. Still, I don't care about Paris. I know you're in Italy, and when the war is over, you'll take me to Tuscany to show me the places where you were.' I look around the dark room, thinking of John lying in the dark, 'Everyone here in town is asking about you,' It takes me a while to remember where he lives, and I finally delete and correct.

'I love and miss you, Georgia.' I sign the letter and look at it. Shall I kiss the paper as she used to do when she loved him?

I bring the letter closer to my lips, kiss it and try to imprint what is left of my lipstick on it, but then I'm once again reminded that he's blind. I'm ashamed of myself for a moment, I almost kissed Henry tonight with those lips.

My fingers forcefully rub the paper, trying to erase my lipstick marks, but it smears until it becomes an ugly stain and I think maybe I should burn this letter and start writing a new one instead, but it's too late, and if I don't give it to him now, I'll lose my nerve.

"It's so hard to be so alone. He has to believe she still loves him," I whisper to the candle as I fold the letter. "I'm not doing it because I miss him. It's for his own good. He misses her letters so much," I keep whispering, hoping no other girl is awake. Still, I don't hold back and kiss the folded paper one more time before I quietly get out of bed and blow out the candle.

"Dear John, even though I didn't receive a letter from you, I know that you will write to me as soon as you can," I stand by his bed and quietly start reading to him, lighting the letter with the lighter I'm holding in my other hand, not stopping to check if he's awake at all.

"Gracie, is that you?"

"Yes, it's me," I keep reading the letter to him, placing my letter-holding hand on his bed, hoping he won't notice my trembling fingers.

"Is that a letter from her?" He puts

his hand on my palm, touching the paper. His fingers are warm.

"Yeah, John, it's from her," I keep reading to him. "Summer will be over soon, and I'm already feeling a chill in the air, remembering how we used to walk together, hugging," I mustn't think of his hand touching me.

"She didn't like it when we hugged in public," he whispers to me. "She used to say that it's embarrassing to hug in front of other people."

"Maybe she misses your hug," I have to move my hand off his bed.

"Maybe," his fingers still touching mine, stroking my hand. I have to think of something else.

"John, what does she look like?"

"Georgia?" He stops moving his fingers.

"Yes."

"She has light hair, slightly curly. And she has bright eyes," I see him move his hands in the dark as if trying to describe her. "We've been together ever since we knew each other, when we were kids," he smiles at me. "I have a picture of her. Do you want to see?"

"Yes, please," I grab the sheet with my fingernails. Why didn't I tell him she didn't want him once that letter had arrived?

"Look in my backpack, in one of the pockets," he gets up and extends his hand, touching my body.

"Sorry, I'm sorry," he leaves his hand on my waist.

"It's okay," I keep standing next to his bed.

"And you, what do you look like?"
I can feel the warmth of his fingers through my uniform.

"I have dark hair, almost straight," I look at him. "And I have dark brown eyes."

"Can I touch your face? to get to know you?"

What shall I reply?

I step back and bend over to his locker, grabbing his backpack, once again looking at the picture of Georgia smiling at me, wearing her summer dress, the same picture I looked at before, when I thought he'd die and that she misses him so much.

"Yes, you can touch my face," I say after a while, returning Georgia's picture into his backpack and locker, approaching him again. She doesn't want him anymore.

His hand fumbles in the air as I bring my face closer, feeling his warm fingers touching my neck gently, then they climb up to my lips, and I let him feel their softness, open my mouth a bit. I mustn't do that; he just wants to get to know the woman he's talking to. My eyes close as his fingers continue to walk up to my nose and then to my cheeks, gently caressing them, and I want to hold his hand but stop myself, gripping the metal frame of the bed tightly. He longs for someone else. I mustn't think of his fingers touching my closed eyes, passing over my lashes and eyebrows like a butterfly fluttering its wings against my skin.

"Your hair is pulled back," he quietly says as he strokes it.

"Yes," I pull back from his touching fingers, take out the hairpins and spread my hair, approach him again, place his hand on my unbound hair, let him feel its smoothness.

"Now I know what you look like," he continues to stroke my hair, goes down with his hand to my neck again, and further down towards my breasts, I mustn't let this go on, he loves someone else, not me.

"I apologize for the previous time, on the road," I'm moving back from his warm hand.

"I have to apologize too, all you wanted to do was show me your boots, and I was angry at you," he leaves his hand in the air. I mustn't get close to his hand again.

"It's okay. I have boots that cover my prosthetic leg."

"So you're no longer Pinocchio? Have you become a real boy?"

"Yes, I became a real boy," I approach him just a bit, lift my legs to his bed, and place his hand on my boot, letting him feel it.

"Pinocchio, you have human legs," his hand caresses the boot and climbs up, touching and stroking my thighs. I want him to keep his hand there, but I know he mustn't go any further.

"Yes, I almost have human legs," I place my hand on his, stroking it back.

"Describe them to me," he leaves his hand on my thigh, gently stroking me, my fingers following his.

"They're brown, and they have laces and buckles," I think of his hand touching me. "And I'm comfortable walking in them," he slides his hand down to the boot and climbs back to my thighs again, I want him to continue, he also knows we shouldn't go on.

"I missed our conversations," he keeps on stroking my legs, and I feel I'm starting to breathe slowly.

"I missed our conversations too. I shouldn't have yelled at you," I get a little closer to him, placing my hand on his waist. Why does he love someone else?

"Did you give the chocolate I threw on the road to the children in the village?" His lips are close to mine.

"I haven't been to the village yet," my fingers caress his cheeks, and I don't tell him that after he left, I walked to the road and threw the bar of crushed chocolate to the weeds, at the side of the road.

"When you go to the village again, will you give it to them?" He brings his lips closer to mine and touches them gently.

"I promise," I cling to him as he kisses me, first gently and then with passion, his fingers caressing my hair, and I try to be as quiet as I can in the dark hall, among the other wounded soldiers sleeping. I can feel his hand stroking my hips as my hands unbutton his shirt, caressing his chest as we kiss deeply, and I breathe heavily. I mustn't do that, If I continue, I wouldn't be able to stop myself.

"I'm sorry," I push him with my hands, trying to calm my breathing quietly and arranging my uniform shirt. Still, the feeling of his hands on my breasts remains, even after I manage to calm myself down.

"I'm sorry, I shouldn't have done this," he puts his hand on my leg again, but I move it away and place it on the sheet, still holding his fingers. We mustn't continue. I won't be able to fall asleep tonight anyway.

"I shouldn't have kissed you. You love someone else."

"Yes, I love someone else," he

removes his hand from mine. "She's waiting for me back home. I was told the ship would arrive soon and that they have to decide whether or not to send me back."

"I have to go. I just came to apologize and read you a letter that arrived from her anyway," I run my finger over my thighs, scratching it with my fingernails, not telling him that this time the ship's for me. I'm tired of running away from this ship.

"Thanks for the letter."

"Good night, John from far away Cold Spring," I force myself to get up from his bed. My bed is waiting for me in the room, with the other girls, covered with a dark, itchy wool blanket.

"Good night, Gracie from Chicago,

the big city beyond the horizon," I hear him whisper, and I'm not replying.

"Gracie?" I still hear him as I walk away.

"Yes?" I stop and turn to him.

"Will you come visit me again?"

"I Promise."

I have to stay away from him. He, too, loves someone else.

✳✳✳

14. Naples.

"Grace, Blanche wants you in her office," Audrey says, entering one of the treatment rooms as I change a soldier's bandage.

"What does she want?"

"She didn't say." Audrey smiles at me and disappears behind the door. My fingers grip the white bandage tightly as I keep wrapping it around his hand.

"You're hurting me." He looks up at me.

"Sorry," I release the bandage and start wrapping it again. What does she want from me?

"Grace, how are you doing here, among all the other nurses?" She looks at me as I stand tall and tense in her office.

"I'm doing fine, Head Nurse Blanche."

"How are you managing after assisting in the German pilot's surgery."

"I'm doing fine here." I don't want to mention that Audrey has been calling me a German-lover since the day I started taking care of Harald. Some of the soldiers call me that as well.

"Well, I'm happy to hear that. Audrey is a good nurse, and works by to the book."

"Yes." I examine the bench in the garden overlooking the sea, I can see it from the window of her office.

"It's a shame all my nurses don't follow the rules like she does."

"Yes, Head Nurse Blanche."

"Do you have anything to tell me about the jeeps that disappeared from my hospital parking lot at night?"

"No, Head Nurse Blanche." I keep looking straight ahead. What would she do to me if she found out?

"You know, Grace..."

"Yes, Head Nurse Blanche," I say as she keeps talking.

"There are always those who think they know better than others, that they can always manage on their own."

"Yes, Head Nurse Blanche."

"Well, those who think that are wrong."

"Yes, Head Nurse Blanche." What does she mean? Is she going to punish me? I keep my head up and look through her window.

"Grace, early tomorrow morning you will accompany one of our trucks to Naples, and help the driver with the medical supplies."

"Why?" I look at her for the first time since entering her office. As usual, she's busy with the lists of names placed on the table in front of her.

"Because that's what intern nurses do – the dirty jobs no one else wants. Maybe that's what you deserve as a reminder, since you seem to have forgotten, that this here is the US Army and you can't do whatever you want."

"Yes, Head Nurse Blanche."

"Now get out my office."

"Yes, Head Nurse Blanche," I answer her and turn around. It seems as though she'll never be happy with me.

"Grace?" she calls after me. I turn around and see her looking up from the page she's holding.

"Yes, Head Nurse Blanche?"

"I appreciate people who keep their humanity during wartime, like those who change bandages for wounded German soldiers after a senior nurse refuses to take care of him."

"Thank you, Head Nurse Blanche."

"That'll be all. You can close the door behind you." She returns to her papers.

"Yes, Head Nurse Blanche." I walk out slowly and close the door behind me. At least there are no severe consequences to my actions.

"I'm to escort you on the drive to Naples," I tell the truck driver standing in the parking lot, smoking and rubbing his hands to keep warm.

It's early dawn. He mutters something under his breath, clearly displeased about them sending him a woman with a cane. He probably thinks he'll have to do all the work himself. He gets in the truck and starts the engine. Honestly, I don't care what he thinks. If this is Blanche's way of punishing me, I can live with that. I've been through worse than being a companion to an unpleasant truck driver, I think to myself. I get inside the truck and slam the metal door behind me.

"To Naples" reads the road sign placed by the American army. Next to it is another sign indicating that the road and its surroundings have been cleared of mines and bomb remnants. Both signs are attached to a wooden pole above a sign that reads 'Naples' in German. Below it is a bullet-hole-riddled Italian sign, 'Napoli.

"It's going to take us a while, the road is badly damaged," the driver finally says after driving in silence for a while, but I don't answer him, I just look at the potholes on the road and try to remember the only other time I drove this way. Back then I was coming from the other direction, from Naples to the front. It was when I had just arrived in Italy, and the war still seemed so exciting. Only a few months have passed since then, but the road seems so different to me.

I look around at the trees and road signs. Still, I can't seem to remember the road. Maybe it's because I was too busy looking at the soldiers sitting next to me in the back of the army truck. I was assigned as a nurse to an infantry brigade on its way north to fight the Germans. It seems to me that a whole life has passed since then.

"Hey there, newbies," a sergeant wearing a dust-covered uniform shouted when he saw us trying to find our way through the crowded Naples port a few months ago. It was already noon, long after we disembarked from the ship, and we had been trying to find our way through the commotion around us. I think it was right after I gave all my cigarettes to the begging children, since I remember the sergeant driving them away, but I don't remember clearly now.

"Yes, sir," the new female soldier and I answered, approaching him and holding our duffelbags tightly.

"Throw your lifejacket there," he instructed us and pointed to a pile of yellow lifejackets lying on the platform.

"Yes, sir," I answered and rushed to remove the lifejacket, placing it on the top of the pile.

"Do you have your documents?" he shouted, his voice trying to overcome the engine noise of several Sherman tanks that had descended to the dock from a tank carrier, and rolled by us with deafening noise.

"Yes, sir," I shouted back and handed him the folded papers in my pocket.

"Wait there," he instructed us after a moment, pointing to a corner of the dock. We dragged our duffelbags next to a pile of diesel-smelling barrels and stood there watching the neverending convoys of trucks full of soldiers and tanks that kept unloading from the landing ships.

Every now and then I looked at
the other female soldier: she wore
a clean white nurse's uniform
like mine, and she too appeared
unbothered by the noise and
vehicles passing around us.

"Hey nurses, will you take care of us
if we get injured?" I heard a voice
and looked up at a group of soldiers
sitting in the back of an army truck
that had been unloaded from one
of the ships. I smiled at them in
response.

"And what about us?" I heard a
few soldiers from another truck.
They smiled at us under the green
helmets they were wearing, but I
didn't have the courage to answer
them.

"Hey you, nurses, the new ones,"
the sergeant approached us and we
both stood up straight.

"Yes, sir."

"There's a problem with your transportation north to the front lines. All vehicles and drivers have been taken by another division."

"Yes, sir," we both said, not knowing what else we could do.

"Let's arrange a ride for you to the war zone. Follow me."

"Yes, sir," we said at the same time and grabbed our duffelbags, rushing after him as he walked between the transport trucks.

"After me." Now he was talking to one of the truck drivers, showing him our papers as we stood there waiting.

"You two, get on this truck," he instructed us while he climbed into the back of the truck.

"Good morning, Infantry Brigade 141," he said to the soldiers sitting in the back of the truck.

"Good morning, Sergeant," they answered him at the same time, straightening up.

"Joining you are two lovely guests traveling north to the front lines."

"Yes, sergeant."

"Treat them nicely."

"Yes, sergeant."

"You two," he turned to us, "where are you from?"

"Sergeant, I'm from Chicago," I shouted as another tank convoy passed by us, shaking the truck.

"Sergeant, I'm from New York," the other nurse answered him.

"That's great. Chicago, New York, I hope you have a safe journey and save a lot of lives in this bloody war." He helped us lift our duffelbags onto the back of the truck, and disappeared behind the other armored vehicles standing on the platform, waiting for their drive up north.

"Miss New York, please sit down." One of the soldiers got up and made room for the nurse on the wooden bench at the back of the truck.

"Miss Chicago, please sit." Another soldier smiled at me under his helmet and moved, making room for me too. I sat down, huddled between them. I could smell the sweat wafting from their army uniforms, the result of the long voyage at sea. I probably smell that way too, I thought to myself.

More and more army trucks joined the convoy, until it seemed like the whole port was full of them. I looked around the truck and noticed the soldiers staring at us curiously, so I lowered my gaze.

"Where are you going?" the other nurse asked them.

"We're on our way to conquer Rome," they answered her and laughed. "And you?"

"We're on our way to a field hospital near the front lines," I answered, looking up and examining their uniform.

"Are you new here?" One of the soldiers asked me.

"Yes, and what about you?" I looked into his black eyes.

"Yes, we're here as reinforcements."

"Straight from America?"

"Straight from faraway America." He smiled at me.

"Me too." I smiled back at him.

"I'm also here as reinforcements," the other nurse said.

"We're the reinforcements everyone's been waiting for. We've come to beat the Germans and finish the war," one of the soldiers said to her and laughed.

"We'll be celebrating Thanksgiving in Berlin," another one joined in.

"The Germans should consider surrendering before your arrival," she smiled at them.

"Move out," shouted one of the commanders standing on the dock, and the convoy of trucks began to slowly drive away from the port and onto the road along the coastline, moving away from the city. The townhouses kept getting smaller behind us until they became tiny dots in the horizon, like a pile of shells spilling into the blue bay.

Suddenly the road got rougher, due to the potholes probably caused by passing tanks and cannon shells that ruined the asphalt. This caused the truck to drive slower, and as for me, I kept my gaze on the green fields and trees until I saw it.

The tank was lying on the side of the road, black and sooty, its cannon pointing towards the ground as if surrendering to the war. I could still see the black German iron cross painted on the sides of the tank.

The other soldiers also followed the tank with their gaze until it disappeared from their view, but after a while another damaged tank appeared on the side of the road along with a destroyed American tank. I looked at the faces of the soldiers sitting on the wooden bench in front of me.

Serious looks replaced the smiles they'd given us at the beginning of the drive. Their eyes that had been focused on the other nurse's lips until now were surveying the surrounding fields, while their hands gripped their guns a little tighter.

The truck slowed down as we passed by another damaged tank blocking a part of the road, the American star still visible on the front of its destroyed turret. The soldiers stared at it intently, even as the truck continued on its way. No one was smiling anymore.

"Where are you from?" I asked the soldiers sitting in front of me.

"Atlanta," one of them replied, turning his gaze away from the wreckage and facing me. "Charlotte, North Carolina," continued the one sitting next to him. "Charleston," the next added, "Jacksonville." One by one, they said the names of their hometowns in an endless list I couldn't possibly remember, and slowly the smiles returned to their faces.

"Please, Miss Chicago," the soldier who had made room for me earlier pulled a box of cigarettes from his uniform pocket and offered me one. "Thanks," I said, and took a cigarette in order to be polite, not telling him I don't smoke.

"Keep the pack," he smiled at me as I handed him the box back.

"Thanks, but it's yours."

"After we kill all the Germans, we'll have as many cigarettes as we want," he said, and everyone nodded in agreement as I leaned towards his outstretched hand holding the metal lighter.

"Maybe you'll need them," I said, and tried not to cough as I inhaled the bitter smoke.

"Please take them so you have a souvenir from me." He took out a pen and wrote his name on the box of cigarettes. "And I'll have a reason to come visit you." He smiled at me. I smiled back at him, stuffing the cigarettes in my pocket and examining his face, which was barely visible under the green helmet he wore.

"Take mine as well," another soldier pulled a box of cigarettes out of his uniform pocket, wrote his name on it, and handed it to me.

"And mine." More soldiers added their names to the cigarette boxes they handed to me.

"Miss New York, do you want a cigarette?" Some soldiers turned to the other nurse, and she laughed and refused them. Still, they didn't give up and kept talking to her, offering to marry her when the war was over and promising to visit. I looked at the road and the destroyed tanks that occasionally appeared on the side of the road.

"This is where your hospital is,

behind the hill," the truck driver shouted to us as he stopped the truck on the side of the road. We rushed to get out, so as not to delay the endless convoy of trucks on their way to the front.

"Good luck, Miss New York; good luck, Miss Chicago," the soldiers on the truck exclaimed. The soldier with the dark eyes just nodded his head without saying a word. I nodded back, saying goodbye to him.

"Don't forget us," the soldier with the boyish face added while smiling at the other nurse.

"We're waiting for you," she said, and waved goodbye as the truck continued on its way.

We both stood there waving

goodbye as the trucks passed us one by one.

"See you in Berlin," some of them shouted to us, and I smiled at them, trying not to think about the burned American tanks I'd seen on the road.

Finally the last truck in the convoy went by, and the quiet fields around us replaced the noise of the engines and dust. We stood alone next to a road sign full of bullet holes, looking for the right way to the hospital.

I bent down and put my duffelbag back on my shoulders, and two boxes of cigarettes fell on the ground. I picked them up and looked at the names written on them. What if they did get wounded and ended up at the hospital? Would I be able to save their lives?

"What are you doing?" she asked me as I walked to the side of the road.

"Nothing," I answered as I took the cigarette boxes out of my uniform pockets and threw them as far as I could into the bushes by the side of the road.

"Aren't those the cigarette boxes they gave you as a present?" she asked.

"I don't smoke," I said to her and looked at the empty road, praying silently they would never have a reason to arrive at the hospital. I had to tell them I was just an intern nurse.

"I thought there was a shortage of cigarettes."

"You heard what they said. After they kill all the Germans, they will have as many cigarettes as they want," I answered, and watched her light a cigarette from one of the boxes the soldiers had given her, even though she'd claimed she didn't smoke.

Two days later, the battle of Rome began in the mountains. The other nurse cracked under the pressure of the neverending stream of wounded and couldn't function anymore. They evacuated her, and I continued my job in the operating tent all by myself.

Although I tried to recognize their faces while examining every wounded soldier, I couldn't remember any of them.

Maybe the fact that I had thrown their cigarette boxes into the bushes had kept them from coming to visit me after all.

Maybe I should have cracked under the pressure as well, then I would have been evacuated back home. But that was a long time ago, in a different lifetime. Now I'm on my way to Naples on the medical supply truck.

"Want a cigarette?" the truck driver asks me as I stare out the window. The road is still badly damaged and full of potholes, but the wrecked tanks lying on the side of the road are gone. Someone must have transferred them along with the rest of the war wreckage. Maybe my leg ended up there as well.

"Want a cigarette?" the driver asks me again, and I turn my gaze towards him.

"Yes, thank you."

"We'll get to town soon." He hands me the lit lighter, and I lean towards his hand, inhaling the bitter smoke and thanking him.

"How were you injured?" he asks.

"A plane."

"During the attack on the hospital?"

"No, before that."

"Was it painful?"

"War is a painful thing, isn't it?"

"Yes, war is a painful thing," he agrees.

"Have you been here long?" I ask him.

"Two and a half years. I haven't

been home in two and a half years, is that a long time?"

"Yes, two and a half years is a long time." I exhale the smoke out the truck's open window.

For a few minutes we slow down, driving after a convoy of refugees headed south on the main road. I want to give them something, but I have nothing, so I just watch them walk slowly, their clothes covered with dirt. For a moment I see a family walking among the crowd; the woman is holding a suitcase, and next to her is a man in a suit that must have meant something back in the day, carrying a little girl in his arms. They don't stop, ignoring us as the truck passes them on the road, they just move a little to the side, continuing their neverending journey. The little girl in his arms looks at me and smiles with her white teeth, and I avert my eyes.

"It's their fault they joined Hitler and let the fascists rule them," the truck driver says to me.

"Yes, it's their fault," I answer and think of Francesca's husband, who was forced to enlist in the army by the Fascists. What would I have done had I been in their shoes?

"May I?" I ask him a few minutes later as we continue on the road, leaving the refugees behind us. I point at a photo of a smiling woman tucked in the dashboard of his truck.

"Yes, of course" he answers and hands me the picture. I look into the woman's happy eyes, turn the photo and read 'Juliana, 1941.'

"She's beautiful."

"I'm a lucky man, she's waiting for me at home, we'll get married when I come back."

"Does she write to you?"

"All the time."

"You're a lucky man," I say, and toss the cigarette out of the window, looking at the Naples townhouses that look like a pile of colored seashells spilling towards the blue bay.

***

At the end of the day, after we fill the truck with medical supplies and drive back from the supply base near Naples, I ask the driver to make a detour and pass through the port.

"Why do you want to go through the port?"

"Just feeling nostalgic, I was there not so long ago and wanted to see it again."

"Before the war?" he asks. "The port has really changed since then. The Germans destroyed it."

"No, I've never been to Italy before the war." I look around as we drive through the city. The narrow streets are no longer full of brick fragments from collapsed buildings as they were the last time I passed here. More people are walking the streets, and I can see the clotheslines stretched between the buildings filled with colorful laundry drying in the autumn sun. But there are still damaged buildings everywhere, some with a mere wall left standing, and some missing their façade, showing remnants of broken furniture.

"They shouldn't have fought us," the driver says, glancing at a ruined wall. But I don't answer, I just look around for the children I saw when I first arrived here, the ones who snatched the cigarette boxes from me.

At the entrance to the port is a new gate with a guard. The port seems to be in order and not too busy. There are no longer damaged ships laying in the water near the docks, with their red bellies towards the sky. And the water, once stained with huge black spots of oil and fuel, has returned to its usual greenish color. The cranes that were in the water have been taken out, and soldiers in coveralls were now working to repair them, illuminating the afternoon with welding sparks that flew into the water like fireworks.

"Please stop," I ask him, and get out of the truck right as he parks it. I walk carefully towards the green water. Everything has changed so much. The last time I was here I had a leg, and everything was so busy and loud.

"Look, the ticket back home," the truck driver stands beside me, pointing to the horizon. A white ship with a large Red Cross painted on its side slowly sails out of the harbor, leaving behind a trail of white foam. The ship's bow faces west towards the setting sun.

294

"What is it?" I ask, even though it seems to me I already know.

"It's a return ticket, my dream, a small injury that will take me home to my beloved lady. The ship carrying the wounded to New York Harbor," he says.

"Yeah, a little injury, that's all it takes," I agree with him, but he keeps talking, and it doesn't seem to me like he's listening.

"The ship just arrived yesterday, and today it's already sailing back. Too bad I'm not standing on its deck waving goodbye," he says, looking at the white ship and the seagulls surrounding it.

I say nothing. I just light another cigarette for myself and take a few steps on the dock, thinking of Head

Nurse Blanche who probably hates me.

"They must have emptied the hospital of the wounded. They're waiting for another major offensive against the Germans in the north," he keeps talking, and I turn to him. John, what about John?

"Did you say something?" he asks me.

"No," I answer and throw the cigarette butt on the ground. "Let's go back." I open the truck door and climb into my seat, rushing the drive to hurry up. What about John?

The way back is taking longer in the dark. The fully-loaded truck drives slowly, as the driver takes care to slow down before any pothole in the road. What will I do if John has gone with the ship today? Why is he driving so slowly? We should have been back at the hospital by now.

"Do you always smoke this much?" the driver asks me when I light another cigarette.

"Yes," I answer and exhale the smoke outside the open window, unable to have a conversation with him. Why didn't I know the ship was coming?

"Can I have one?" he asks, and I give him one, seeing his face by the light of the lighter for a brief moment. I didn't have time to say goodbye to John. Why didn't I go up to say goodbye to him in the morning?

"It's nice to have company driving this way at night," the driver keeps talking and smiling at me.

"Yes, it's nice." I look out the window, trying to locate the village lights and the hospital, but I notice only a few lights in the dark and I can't spot the hospital. When will we get there?

"Good night," I say goodbye to the driver as soon as he stops the truck in the hospital parking lot. Finally I can hear the silence after hours of driving, surrounded by the engine noise and the smell of burnt diesel.

"Good night," I think I hear him reply, but I'm already rushing towards the hospital stairs. I have to find him.

"Where were you? They've been looking for you all day," Audrey asks me. "Even the hospital commander was angry with Blanche when he heard you weren't here. I don't know what she told him."

"I don't know either," I reply to her. I need to get the list of the wounded soldiers that were shipped back.

"Where were you?"

"I went to see refugees."

"What do you mean, 'I went to see refugees'?"

"You wouldn't understand." She also wouldn't understand if I ask her to give me the list of those shipped back home. So I enter the nurses' room, searching for it and seeing it hanging on the wall.

"Please get out. It's my shift now. You can't disturb me right now."

"I need to see something."

"You're bothering me. Please get out."

"I just need a minute, and I'll go."

"Get out of here. You've already done enough damage," she whispers to me and gets up from her table.

"What damage?"

"You wouldn't understand." She smiles at me with her perfect red lips.

"Please," I step back, "I only need a minute."

"Gracie, you used to be a nice person once, and it was worth helping you. Now please stop bothering me." She sits back down at the table and opens the book she's been reading, trying to return to the page that was lost when she got up.

"My name is Grace. You have no right to call me Gracie," I answer her, turn around, and exit the light-filled room into the dark hall. I have to find him.

Bed after bed, I'm walking in the dark, touching the white metal bed frames and looking for him. Most of the beds are empty, and my hands feel the smooth clean sheets waiting for the next wave of wounded to arrive. John's bed is also empty. I didn't even get to say goodbye to him. That can't be right. He's in no condition to be returning home.

I walk as fast as I can, checking the beds in the hall again, looking closely at the sleeping men still in the hall, trying to find John in the dark. I don't want to turn on the light, fearing Audrey will come and kick me out of here. I have to find him.

"John?" I whisper and touch the palm of a wounded man in the third row.

"Um?" I hear him saying. He's not John.

"Sorry, go back to sleep," I touch his shoulder and move to the next bed.

"John?" I whisper to another wounded man who smells a little like John, stroking his fingers.

"Gracie wooden leg?" His fingers caress my hand.

"Yes, it's me, Gracie wooden leg." I stroke his hair.

"Didn't you get on that ship? I thought you left without saying goodbye."

"No, I didn't go," I wipe away a tear, not telling him that's exactly what I thought.

"They read the list in the morning, you were on it, and I heard people asking and searching for you. I sat on the bench in front of the sea all day, and thought you went with the convoy without saying goodbye." He sits up in bed.

"I wouldn't have left without saying goodbye to you." I touch his chest, feeling it through his open hospital shirt.

"Gracie." He touches my hand and brings me closer to him. "Let's do something, let's get out of here."

"Where should we go?" I have to stop touching him even though I can feel his hand gently stroking my hair.

"Let's go somewhere where I'm not an injured soldier, and you're not a nurse."

"It's midnight and it's completely dark outside." I'm holding his hand. We shouldn't.

"What does it matter?" He laughs quietly and gets out of bed. "The night is my companion all the time." He leans over to put on his shoes, touching me by mistake but keeping his hand on my waist. I really shouldn't stand so close to him.

"Come with me, Gracie wooden leg." He stands up, takes my hand, and starts walking through the hall. I follow him, holding his hand tightly.

"I can't see in the dark," I whisper to him as we search for the exit to the garden.

"Then be like me." He feels his way along the wall, still holding my hand.

"But you don't have a wooden leg."

"Right," he holds my hand and pretends to limp, "here, I do now."

"I hate my limp," I whisper to him as we walk in the empty garden outside the hospital even though, there's no longer a reason to whisper.

"But I love it, it makes you special, part of who you are to me," He pauses for a moment, still holding my hand. It seems as though he wants to hug me but changes his mind at the last moment. What have I done? Why did I start this thing with John? Why did I lie to him about the letters?

"Let's go to the sea." I take his hand and walk towards the cliffs and the path that goes down to the shore.

***

15. The Sea.

Once we're at the bottom of the trail, I turn around and look up at the path we just came down from, using our hands to cling to the rocks and each other, being careful not to slip. In the dark I can't really see the path, and the silhouette of the black cliff above us seems so threatening. I gasp and smile at it. We've finally reached the strip of sand leading to the sea.

"Do you hear the sirens? They're singing to us from the sea, inviting us in," John whispers to me.

"We really shouldn't get closer to them. We must stay where we are," I whisper back to him. I'm a cheat and a liar, just like those sirens, but I don't want to lie to him tonight.

"What could possibly happen to us? I'm blind, and you're missing a leg." He takes my hand and begins finding his way towards the waves we hear in the distance. The sand underneath our feet seems bright even in the dark.

"I can't." I release my hand and stand still, looking at his silhouette walking away from me. Why did I bring us here? I'm a cripple.

"Is everything okay? Did I say something wrong?" John stops and turns around, walking back to me. What should I tell him?

"I can't walk on the sand," I finally say.

"Why? It's so pleasant and soft."

"That's exactly the problem," I breathe deeply. I have to face it.

I will always be the handicapped woman, who can't go to the beach, nothing can fix that.

"What's the problem? You don't like sand?"

"I like the sand, I like its touch on my feet and its softness," I say quietly, hoping he won't hear me over the sound of the waves, "but I'm unable to walk on the soft sand."

"Can the sand damage your prosthetic?" He walks towards me.

"No." I don't bother wiping my tears away since he can't see them.

"Or is it the sea water that can damage it?" He gets even closer to me.

"No, I'm just not stable enough on the soft sand. I can't walk on it."

"Come with me." He bends down and takes me in his arms, walking on the soft sand towards the water.

"John, you're crazy, you're injured."

"All I am is blind, so please point me towards the water," he laughs.

"A little to the left," I laugh and wipe away my tears, "you're crazy and blind." I hug his neck and cling to him, feeling his warm body and his breath as he carries me towards the white waves gently hitting the shore.

"Welcome to Italy." He lowers me once we reach the water, and I feel the soft sand and cold water around my legs as he suddenly presses his lips to mine. "You have a pleasant laugh."

His hands grip my waist tightly, and I cling to him, feeling his warm lips against mine. My hand caresses the back of his neck as I kiss him again and again, feeling his hands touching my body and stroking my breasts through my uniform, while his fingers search for the buttons.

Button by button he opens my shirt, and I tremble and breathe heavily at the touch of his warm hands. My hand opens his shirt and caresses his chest, feeling his scars with the tips of my fingers. I remember changing his bandages over those wounds. Back then I thought he was going to die. We have to stop, I have to tell him the truth about the letters and the woman he thinks is waiting for him at home.

"We need to get back," I pull away from him and gasp for air, feeling the cool water on my feet.

"Yes, we have to go back." He doesn't try to kiss me again. "This sea isn't safe for us."

"Will you take me back to reality?"

Without saying a word he hugs me for a few moments, wrapping his warm hands around my body to protect me from the cool night breeze.

"Hold me tight," he lifts me up in his arms again, and I keep stroking his chest, feeling his body through the open hospital shirt.

"Gracie, if you don't point me in the right direction, we'll never reach the cliff," he whispers to me.

"I don't care," I whisper back, resting my head on his chest, inhaling the scent of his body. I'm so pathetic.

"Wait for me here. I'll be right back," I say to him as we get back to the top of the cliff and sit down on the white bench overlooking the black sea. I want to be with him a little longer, even though he's probably dreaming of another woman, but we're both shaking in our wet clothes.

I quickly enter the dark building, climb into the nurses' bedroom and take my woolen blanket with me. All the other nurses are asleep. Only Audrey's bed is empty, she's probably on call. I hope she's not looking for John.

"Gracie, I'm sorry I kissed you like that," he says when I sit close to him and cover us both with the blanket. "I shouldn't have done that."

"It's I who should apologize." I hug myself under the blanket.

"I have to be loyal to the one who's waiting for me at home."

"Yes, she's waiting for you." I know it's time to tell him, but I can't.

"I got carried away. But I have to think about her. She's the one who's waiting for me."

"What if she wasn't?" I take a deep breath.

"I don't know, Gracie, I don't know." I feel his warm body under the blanket, but I suddenly lose my courage.

"Sometimes I think we're all wanderers in this war, moving around from place to place, without meaning," I say and close my eyes. Now I'm thinking how it might have been better for him or me to go back home. I wish we could just keep the good memories between us and leave the lies behind.

His hands wrap around my cold body and hug me, but we don't kiss this time, and I struggle to keep my eyes open and not fall asleep. No one has hugged me this way in a very long time.

"Gracie, are you awake?"

"Yes, John, I'm awake." I open my eyes for a moment, still resting my head on his chest.

"I think someone engraved an airplane onto this bench. I can feel it with my fingertips. I've been trying to figure out what it is for a few minutes."

"He must have wanted to fly to the stars," I whisper to him, but he doesn't answer me.

"John, are you asleep?"

"No, Gracie."

"I feel lost."

"Why?"

"I can't say."

"Not to even a blind soldier?"

"Not to even a blind soldier. I don't really know what to do."

"Don't worry. You'll find the answer."

"I'm not so sure anymore."

"Do you remember I told you about the clock at Central Station in New York?"

"Yes."

"It's right above the information booth, right in the center of the hall," he slowly whispers. "I remember when I was a kid, every time I came to the big city with my parents I would look at the golden clock and all the people standing in front of the woman behind the information desk. Once I asked my mother who she was," he says, and I find his voice so pleasant. "She told me the woman behind the counter was a great magician who had the answer to every question you could possibly think of. And all the people in line were there because they were waiting for her answers."

"Do you think she'll know the answer to my questions?" I want to touch his body under the blanket.

"If you suddenly feel lost, you can always go there and ask her. I'm sure she'll have the answer." His warm body makes me feel comfortable, and I struggle to keep my eyes from closing.

"I feel like I should have said some things that went unsaid, and now it's too late."

"I feel like I'm cheating on her."

"Don't feel that way. You haven't done anything wrong."

"I seduced you."

"I wanted to be seduced, and in any case, I'm the liar and the cheater."

"Me too. I need to write to Georgia and tell her that I've changed."

"Yes, you should write to Georgia." I'm a liar and a coward, and I don't have the courage to tell him that I faked the letters from Georgia. I'll tell him tomorrow. Now I'm just going to close my eyes for a few minutes.

What's the time? I look at the sky, which is turning reddish. Did I fall asleep?

"John, are you awake?"

"Yes, Gracie, I'm awake."

"We need to go back inside. They'll probably be looking for you soon, not knowing where you went. And I need to start my shift. New wounded soldiers will be coming in from the front. I have to be ready for them."

I want him to say something or to kiss me, but he says nothing, he just puts his hand on my shoulder and I feel his warm fingers through my rough uniform. Maybe I should have been the one to kiss him or say something. I should have probably said a lot of things to him.

On the way inside, as we cross the driveway, I stop for a moment on the hospital stairs and look back. I can see some army ambulances approaching on the main road, but in the morning light they look almost black, their front lights shining like yellow flashlight eyes.

***

"Cold Spring, New York? Is there anyone here from Cold Spring, New York? Does anyone know someone from there? Cold Spring, New York?" We're standing at the entrance to the hall, as I hear a newly-wounded soldier shouting. He's supporting himself with crutches and walking between the beds, asking loudly about Cold Spring, New York. I suddenly freeze.

"I think John is from there. John?" I hear Audrey's voice.

She helps the wounded soldier get settled into his new bed and places his backpack in the metal locker. "John?" She gets up and turns to us, looking at John and me.

"Yes, I'm from there, John Miller," he answers the soldier, and I feel his fingers letting go of my shoulder.

"John Miller? How are you? I haven't heard from you in so long. What happened to you? Where were you injured? Edgar Foster, remember me? I was two years under you in high school. I remember you joined the army in the first wave." He approaches John with his crutches, making his way between the beds and extending his hand to shake John's. I make room for him and move back, watching Edgar's hand as it remains raised in the air, while he looks at John. Finally he realizes John is unable to see him. I have to stay away, let them talk.

"I remember you," John smiles at him and extends his hand in the air towards the voice, "so you're here as well? When did you join this bloody war? How were you injured?"

"I'm new here, it's just my rotten luck, a bullet in the foot from a

German sniper, but the doctors say I'll fully recover."

"And how are things at home? How's my Georgia?"

"Georgia? Your fiancée Georgia? Didn't you hear?" Edgar keeps talking. "She's marrying someone else, some substitute teacher who came from the city because of the war, Gerard something, I don't even remember his last name."

***

"Georgia Griffin?" John pauses the handshake. I want to run out of the hall, my head full of the sounds of beating drums.

"Yeah, Georgia, from your class, I

remember her. You were together all the time. She told everyone you broke up and that she wrote to you about it, and now she's with someone else."

"I don't understand," I hear John. I must escape this place, but I can't move, my hands are trying to support myself by holding one of the iron beds.

"Didn't you know? I'm so sorry," the wounded soldier, I think his name is Edgar, looks around as if searching for something to say.

"I don't understand." John turns in my direction, looking at me through the sunglasses he's wearing.

What should I tell him?

"Maybe she wrote to you and the letter didn't arrive? You know some letters are lost. We're at war, after all," I say, and try to get closer to him. It seems to me that Edgar and the other wounded men in the hall are looking at us. I have to get out of here.

"But you've been reading me letters from her that she sent recently. She wrote about the coming fall, preparations for Thanksgiving, she wrote that she misses me, I don't understand." He keeps looking in my direction, and I look around, searching for help, but the hall is empty of nurses. Even Audrey has left me alone with my lies. Only Edgar, John and the other soldiers are looking at me as I stand in front of them in the center of the hall, feeling as if I'm being hit by a ton of bricks as I search for the right words.

"Dear John," I hear Audrey's voice behind my back and turn around. She's standing at the entrance to the hall, reading a letter.

"It's been so long since I've written to you," she continues to read, and I already know by heart what the following lines are. "There's no easy way to say this, but I've met someone else, and we're together... Should I continue?" She approaches John, and I take a step back, holding onto another bed frame.

"Grace, what's going on here?" he asks me, but I'm out of words.

"I'll keep reading then," Audrey smiles at me with her red lips. "The distance between us, the longing, and the loneliness were unbearable for me. I've met someone else who was there by my side during those difficult times. I'm so sorry, but we're together now. You will always be special to me. Bye, Georgia," Audrey reads the last line slowly.

"John, Georgia wrote to you," Audrey keeps talking to him, ignoring me. "But Gracie here hid the letters from you." She puts Georgia's letters in his hand, and I want to turn around and run from this place, but I'm trapped between the iron beds and the peering eyes of the wounded soldiers.

"But why? I don't understand?" He turns to me, and I can see the tears flowing from his eyes through the sunglasses.

How can I explain to him that I did this to protect him when he was lying in bed, severely injured? I try to find the right words.

"I'll tell you why," I hear Audrey's voice again. "Because she wants you to love her."

"That's not true," I say, but Audrey gets even closer to him, standing by his side as I take another step back.

"Are you still trying to decide who to believe?" she says to John. "Ask your soldier friend from Cold Spring to read you Georgia's letters."

"I don't understand why." He continues to stand there, holding the letters in his hand and looking in my direction. I want to wipe the tears coming down his cheeks, to explain that I care about him, but I can't, Audrey is holding his hand now.

"All she wants is for people like you to love her," she continues, "but don't worry." She looks at me for a moment and smiles. "You're not the only one. Has she told you yet that she's dating a pilot who shows her his plane at nights?"

It seems to me the entire hall is quiet now and that everyone is staring at me. Even the newly-wounded soldiers who just arrived are whispering back and forth with the older ones, asking them about the nurse standing in the center of the hall with her hands shaking.

"Are you seeing someone else? Is that where my glasses came from?" John turns in the direction he thinks I am, but I'm not there anymore, I'm walking away, I need to get out of here.

"You're not the only one she's been lying to, and neither is the pilot,"

Audrey strokes his hand. "She's been lying to me as well. She told she has someone waiting for her at home, but no one ever writes her. She took your letters and told me they were hers."

"Is that true?" he speaks into the empty air near him, the spot where I was just standing, and I hear a loud noise as John steps on the sunglasses, crushing them with his foot. Why didn't I return the letters? I must explain to him. He must know my feelings for him.

"I didn't want you to get hurt. You were so wounded," I manage to get the words out of my mouth, and he looks at me, surprised at how far away I have gone.

"You didn't want me to get hurt so you hurt me even more by lying to me? I thought you were my friend."

"I am your friend," I struggle to get the words out.

"I thought she was my friend too, at first," Audrey interrupts me. "Until I realized who she really was."

"I think I don't have to be afraid of going home anymore," he says in my direction. "No one is waiting for me anymore, and the only one who's been by my side through it all did it out of pity, lying to me all this time."

"John, please." I start to walk towards him.

"Don't come near me."

"John, please, let me explain. I'm not seeing anyone else." I keep walking, ignoring the looks from the other wounded and their whispers, trying to get closer to him. It seems as though one of the soldiers is trying to trip me and I almost stumble, grabbing on to the metal bed frame and John's hand so as not to fall.

"Don't touch me," he whispers to me, "your lies and pity are the worst thing I could have asked for. Luckily I'm blind and can't see the look in your eyes."

***

My room, I'll go to my room, there's a wall I can peel there. I turn around and limp to the exit, holding the beds' metal frames while walking, afraid someone will make me stumble. Step by step I advance towards the entrance in the quiet hall while keeping my eyes on the floor. Ignore all the looks and the whispers burning my back. The most important thing is to escape from here. I climb the stairs to the second floor, enter the nurses' bedroom and freeze. Audrey's revenge is visible here as well.

The metal locker next to my bed is open, and all its contents are scattered on the floor. She has ripped my notebook, thrown the crumpled pieces of paper along with my clothes on the floor, and stepped all over them with her shoes. My pink lipstick is smeared on the floor, creating an ugly stain, and the wooden stick I got from Francesca lies broken in pieces. Fighting tears, I look at my leather boots, the ones that hide my wooden leg. Each of them has a large cut from a sharp knife, and they lie on my white bedsheets as if they were bodies whose life-saving surgery had failed.

What did I do to her? Why does she hate me so much?

I leave of the room, unable to stay inside. I must find out why she did this. I've already ruined everything, and it doesn't matter to me anymore. I must find her and find out. I carefully go down the stairs, occasionally wiping the tears, being careful not to slip, but I don't dare re-enter the hall. Everyone there knows what happened just a few minutes ago. I'm the one to blame, and they will blame and curse me. I stand at the entrance and peek inside the hall, but she's no longer there. I have to find her.

The hospital garden is almost empty. Only a few wounded choose to go outside after the sun has disappeared, making way for clouds that cover the sky. Where can she be?

"Why do you hate me so much?" I finally ask her, standing, shaking in front of her. She's in my spot, sitting on the wooden board Francesca and I laid on the ground a few days ago in order to avoid getting wet from the dirt. She's sitting in my hiding spot, leaning against the shed wall.

"I was wondering when you'd get here, Pinocchio," she looks up at me and exhales the cigarette smoke.

"Why? Why do you hate me so much?"

"Yeah, I thought about it. You're right. I really do hate you." She inhales from the cigarette in her hand.

"What did I do to you?" I stand in front of her, my body shaking, and I can feel the tears streaming down my cheeks. "You used to take care of me, you used to be nice to me."

"Yeah, back then, when you were so injured and helpless, you were nice back then," she looks up at the clouds. "Back then, it was worth being nice to you."

"What changed? That I wanted to recover and stop being helpless? Aren't we nurses supposed to be compassionate towards each other?" I wipe my eyes, wanting to sit but unable to bring myself so close to her.

"I thought we already agreed that we don't have to keep the oath and everything we promised ourselves before we came to this place. Aren't we at war?"

"Why are we at war?"

"Don't you understand?" She looks at me and exhales the smoke towards me again, and I keep standing there looking at her, saying absolutely nothing.

"It's all about what you choose, Pinocchio," she continues. "In the beginning you were wounded and nice because you needed me, but then, when you started to recover, you started choosing, and you never chose my side."

"What are you talking about?"

"Do you really not understand?" She takes scissors out of her dress pocket and throws them in the mud. "This is my gift for your boots, because you always choose the other side."

"Which other side?"

"You chose the cursing Italian who hates me, and you chose John."

"What about John?" I wipe my cheeks again.

"He was my wounded soldier, but you stole him from me, taking care of him at night, making him like you more than me."

"But he was blind and almost dead. Someone had to take care of him."

"Yes, and that someone was me. I'm the senior nurse, and I took care of him until you showed up, like a compassionate angel, and at the end of the day they all like you more than me." She threw her cigarette into the mud. "And what about Henry?"

"What about Henry?"

"I wanted him, and he preferred you."

"All the other girls wanted him, but you chose to hate me for it?" I yell at her. "Couldn't you hate someone else?"

"All the other girls want him, that's right," she speaks to me indifferently. "But in the end, he chose to invite you to his jeep. The lame intern in the simple khaki uniform." She looks at me and I see she has tears on her cheek. "What exactly did you say to him that he chose you? There's nothing to you but lies. "

"I'm sorry Henry invited me."

"You don't feel sorry Henry invited you, you're always nice to everyone, lying to them as you see fit, and in the end they like you. And you always choose the ones I care for, making them like you more. You even treated the German pilot with a smile on your face."

"But you had asked me to take care of him," I shout at her, trying not to shake.

"I didn't ask you," she shouts back at me. "He was supposed to die, he's our enemy, don't you understand? But you took care of him and kept him alive. You chose Francesca the Italian, the blind man likes you more, the pilot likes you more, even the dying German likes you more. In the end, that's how it is, you're either with me or against me. And you're definitely not with me."

"Really?" I scream at her. "Do you think everyone likes me? In case you hadn't notice, I am an amputee without a leg," I ignore the tears on my cheeks, "and if you hadn't noticed, John hates me, and Henry probably doesn't like me at all, and yes, I lie to everyone. I'm a liar. What is there to like about me anyways?" I support myself leaning against the wall, struggling to stay upright.

"You're right. There really is nothing to like about you. I don't understand how you can even tolerate yourself." She turns away from me and lights another cigarette for herself.

"Americana, stop," she follows me.

"Leave me alone," I yell at her and keep walking, trying to get away from her.

"Americana, you can't go there," she continues to shout at me.

"It's none of your business. It's between him and me." I look back for a moment and see her behind me, her black dress fluttering in the wind. "Go back to your village." I turn my back on her and approach the rocks. It's time for me to search for the cross I threw into the sea back then.

"Americana, it's dangerous. You can fall."

"That's none of your business." I start walking down the rocks. It's time I give up the path that goes down to the beach. It would have been better if I hadn't gone down there last night with John.

"Americana, stop," she yells at me, but I don't listen to her. I bend down and hold onto the smooth rocks, sitting at the edge of the cliff and looking at the angry gray waves below.

"What did I do wrong to you? Didn't I try hard enough to keep him alive? Didn't I care enough about him? What did I do so wrong that you punish me over and over?" I scream at the waves below me.

"Americana, be careful." I hear her, but I don't care anymore. I'm tired of getting up and falling, only to get up and fall again.

"Why is this so hard?" I shout at the seagulls screaming above me.

"Because that's how it is, Americana, it's hard sometimes," she yells at me. "Nothing is waiting for you there."

"I don't care," I turn around and yell at her, looking at her holding the hem of her dress with her hands while the wind hits her. "Nothing is waiting for me here too. I'm a liar."

"Americana, we're all liars," she stands up and shouts back at me.

"Really, la vedova en moto? What are you lying about?"

"Everything, Americana, I lie about everything." She looks at me and comes one step closer.

"I'm a liar, and I'm disabled, and

I'm afraid to go home," I shout at her, standing and taking another step towards the edge. The sound of the waves at the bottom of the cliff invite me to join them.

"I'm lying to myself that my husband will come back one day," I hear her.

"You don't know that," I answer without turning my head, still looking at the white foam and the waves.

"You don't know that either," I hear her.

"Who could ever love me like this?" I turn to her and scream, trying to overcome the noise of the wind and the waves. "Who would want a crippled woman without a leg?" I fold and collapse on the sharp rock at the end of the cliff. "Who would want me?" I sit on the rocks and cry. "I'll never have someone that loves me."

"Shhh... Americana, it's okay," she approaches and bends over me, hugging me with her warm arms.

"How am I going to get back home like this?" I sob. "What I've done is so awful." I turn around and scream to the sea, wanting to break free from her arms that surround me. "All in all, I tried to help him. He was going to die. I wanted people around me to live. I wanted to be a nurse who saves people. Why did I come here at all?" I can't stop weeping.

"Shhh... Americana, it's okay, you're amazing, Americana, you saved a life, and one day you'll find some nice Americano."

"How would anyone like a crippled liar like me?" I look at her through my teary eyes. "I stole his letters and read them to myself, trying to imagine that someone loved me."

"Shhh... Americana, your Americano will come one day."

"You don't know that," I sob into her embrace.

"You're right, Americana, I don't know that." She sits down next to me and holds me tightly. "But I do know one thing, that you're the most special Americana I have ever met, and I know one more thing, that you have to believe that one day the right man will come, as I have to keep believing that one day my husband will return from Russia." She strokes my hair with her fingers, releasing the hairpins, letting my hair flutter in the cold wind. I look at her and notice that she's crying too.

"Everyone hates me, and I'm a liar." I hug her.

"Everyone hates me, and I'm a liar too." She hugs me back. "But don't go to the sea. It is disgusting and cold." She wraps her arms around me, making sure I don't get any closer to the edge of the cliff.

The cold autumn wind continues to whistle around us as we huddle on the rocks above the water. I try to ignore the cries of the seagulls flying over us, screaming and waving their wings as they struggle against the wind.

I lift my head and look down at the gray sea. How will I enter the hospital again, when everyone knows what I've done?

"How will I go back in there?"

"I don't know, Americana."

"For la vedova en moto who always knows what to do, you sure know nothing."

"Yes, Americana, I know nothing too." She gets up and holds my hand, helping me off the ground. We both smile at each other, wipe away our tears and hug as we walk back to the hospital.

Now they can hate us both.

***

16. The Thanksgiving of 1944.

"Lord, Thank you for your blessings over us." Audrey stands in the center of the hall and reads from a page she holds in her hand. "Thank you for saving our lives on the battlefield of Italy." I watch her reading from the entrance. All of the other nurses are gathered around her in front of the wounded sitting in their beds and listening to her. I'm more comfortable standing at the entrance of the hall. I don't usually go inside except during my shifts. I don't want to deal with the looks and curses of the wounded soldiers.

"Lord, Thank you for helping us recover," she continues her prayer, and I can see him from a distance. He's wearing new sunglasses. Probably a gift from Audrey. I wonder what she had exchanged them for.

"Thank you for bringing us together here." I keep looking at them from a distance. I prefer to work in the operating room; the wounded lying on the table, sedated by morphine, don't care about what I've done.

"Thank you for the food you bring to our mouths." She points to the food cart standing beside her. The supply ship was delayed, and no turkey arrived at the hospital. Still, some nurses went to the trouble of decorating the hall with colorful blue, red, and white ribbons. They didn't invite me to join them.

"Thank you, Lord, and may we return home soon." She finishes her prayer, and the wounded nod their heads as the other nurses begin to move between the beds, handing them out the holiday meals. One nurse enters the nurses' station and turns on the radio. Pleasant music spreads through the hall. I like Thanksgiving, even though I have nothing to be thankful for this year.

"Happy Thanksgiving." They smile at each other, and I can see Audrey stroking John's hair, handing him his holiday meal. "Have a good night," they say to them later and leave the hall. They look right past me when they leave, as if I don't exist. Only one of the nurses smiles at me and touches my palm, as if accidentally; they have to prepare for a Thanksgiving party with the pilots.

I've stopped going to the pilots' club, and I don't know whether

Henry is looking for me. I no longer go out to the front stairs to sit with the nurses while they wait for the pilots to visit them either.

I can't go to the party even if I wanted to. The boots Audrey ruined are gone now, she must have thrown them away. I must wait until the nurses leave and then go up to my room.

"Grace," Blanche calls me later from her office, as I walk down the quiet hallway to the nurses' bedroom. I'm going to lie in bed and read a book, marking the pages with dog ears until I fall asleep.

"Yes, Head Nurse Blanche." I enter her room. I have to thank her for the trip to Naples that helped me escape the ship going home, but I'm scared; she must have heard what I did with John.

"Aren't you going out tonight with the other nurses?"

"No, Head Nurse Blanche."

"And may I ask why?"

"I don't think they like me very much, Head Nurse Blanche."

"Since when do you care what others think of you?" She gets up from her chair and turns to a metal cabinet. She opens one of the drawers, pulling out a bottle of whiskey. "You have a lot of things to be thankful for," she looks at me, "like, for example, the ship you miraculously didn't board again." She sits down in her brown chair and pours herself a glass.

"Thank you, Head Nurse Blanche."

"And maybe, despite what you've

done, you should also be thankful for one of the wounded you treated with so much care." She pulls another glass from the drawer of her table and pours me a drink.

"He doesn't want to talk to me anymore, Head Nurse Blanche." I approach the table and take the glass, holding it in my hand. I tried to talk to him several times while he sat in the garden on the bench overlooking the sea, but he pretended not to hear me. The other times I tried, Audrey saw me and asked me to leave. Even at night, when I approached his bed, he pretended to be asleep.

"Since when do you stop yourself from trying to fix something that went wrong?" She raises her glass of whiskey. "Cheers."

"Cheers, thank you, Head Nurse Blanche." I sip the whiskey.

"You know, Grace, it would be nice if you could stay with us a little longer."

"Yes, Head Nurse Blanche."

"So get out of my office and go and have some fun, it's Thanksgiving."

"I don't have too much to be thankful for, Head Nurse Blanche."

"Grace, I received confirmation today that you're one of the permanent nurses on my staff. You no longer need to keep dodging the ship going home."

"Yes, Head Nurse Blanche."

"So you have at least one thing to be thankful for."

"Thank you, Head Nurse Blanche."
I place the glass of whiskey on the
table and leave her room. I have
many other things to try and fix.

"And don't touch my jeeps." I hear
her as I walk down the hall.

"Yes, Head Nurse Blanche."

***

My fingers caress the steering
wheel of the jeep. I've been sitting
here for a long time. Although I
try to listen to the crickets' sounds
out there in the dark, I hear only
the sounds of music and laughter
from inside the hut. Sometimes it
seems to me that I can hear Henry's
laughter amidst all the other voices.
Should I go inside?

The white nurse's dress feels strange on my body. My lips are pale, lipstick-less, they aren't even painted with the simple red lipstick, which Audry had ruined. I hadn't gotten myself a new one, the type of lipstick that would make the pilots gawk at my lips. All I have is a wooden leg and simple shoes, not even boots to hide my prosthetic.

A dress and a wooden leg, that's me.

What will they think when they see me?

I look up at the dark control tower feeling as though it's looking back at me. It's now or never.

I let go of the steering wheel, and get out of the jeep. Maybe I will return humiliated in a few minutes.

Twenty-two steps, and I stand at the entrance of the hut, looking inside.

The club remains as it was, the same flags that hang on the ceiling, the same pilots in khaki uniforms and leather jackets embossed with the squadron emblem, the same nurses dancing in their arms or sitting by the small tables covered in cigarette smoke. Nothing changed, except that everyone was staring at me as I stood at the door.

I can't tell whether they've all stopped talking because of me, but it seems as though the couples have stopped dancing while the music keeps on playing. The nurses sitting by the tables are now looking at me. I need to go inside.

My eyes scan them as I pass by the whispering couples on the dance floor. I notice Henry among them, holding a beautiful girl with wavy gold-colored hair and fair skin; she's from the transportation corps. She hugs him tightly as he whispers something in her ear.

"Just go inside," I say to myself, but I stay standing in the doorway and smile awkwardly. It was a mistake to come here.

Just a few steps. I breathe deeply. I'll sit at the table and drink gin, even if I have to sit here by myself all night. I won't give up. This is me, Grace, with a dress and a wooden leg, and this is what I've decided to do, no matter what. All through the drive here I encouraged myself, again and again, driving slowly through the dark village.

Just a few steps to the small table in the corner of the hut. I start walking.

"Can I ask you to dance?" Henry leaves the transportation girl with the golden hair and walks in my direction.

"I think there's already a lovely lady dancing with you."

"And now someone else will dance with the lovely lady. Can I ask you to dance with me?"

"Not if you're going to pity me."

"Why should I pity you?" He looks into my eyes. "For not wearing lipstick?"

"My lipstick was lost in the war." I hold his arm. Can I trust him?

"You're lovely with or without lipstick." He puts his hand on my waist and leads me to the small dance floor. I place my hands on the back of his neck and get closer to him, smelling his cologne, but before I close my eyes and let myself go with the music, I see Audrey walking out of the hut. She probably doesn't want to be in the same room with me. We haven't spoken at all since that day.

"Thanks," I whisper to him later as we dance between the couples. He gently leads me through the dance, ignoring my limp as if it doesn't exist.

"What?"

"Nothing," I say to him and let myself open my eyes.

"Can I dance with your girl?" I hear someone say and see another pilot standing next to us.

"Would you like to dance with him?" Henry asks for my permission. I smile at him and say thanks as he walks away to the other girl. I hold the pilot's hands and dance with him, and then another, and another, until my legs hurt. Still, I don't care, the pain can wait. One dance is followed by another as glass after glass of gin is served to me by the pilots. I focus on the music and move to its rhythm and enjoy the hands holding my body, ignoring the looks around me until I gasp and ache. I say goodbye to the last handsome pilot dancing with me and go stand in the corner, letting myself have a little rest. The dancing couples are no longer looking at me, and neither are the women sitting by the tables. They were once again smiling at the pilots around them. I look down at my wooden leg. I have so much more to fix.

"See you later," I finally say to Henry from a distance, waving at him as I turn to the door.

"Grace, wait." He leaves the golden-haired girl hugging him and walks over to me. "I'll take you back."

"No thanks, I have a jeep, and you have a girl to dance with."

"You already know me," he smiles. "You know how I am with women."

"Yeah, I already know you," I smile back at him and walk towards the door, but suddenly I stop and turn around. Walking over to him and grabbing his waist, I say to him: "You know, you have to stop trying to prove to everyone who you are and how you are with women. You're a good man, and you're a good pilot, and you've paid enough in this war. We've all paid enough. I gave up my leg, and I gave up the idea that anyone will ever want me again. But we're allowed to go back home and be who we are."

"You have a lot of grace in you," he smiles at me, and it seems he wants to kiss me, but he needs to kiss someone else instead.

"This war will end one day," I continue to hold him, "and you'll go back home to the same train station you left three years ago. Your dad's black Cadillac, the one you stole, will be waiting for you, and you'll get in and drive home. Your dad should be proud of you and everything you've done in this war. He should be proud of the insignia on your shoulders." I look up and smile at him, touching the medals on his chest with my fingers. "And you'll go to Betty's house, you'll knock on her door, holding flowers, and ask her to go out with you. And it'll be her win if she accepts your invitation. There's nothing wrong with you, and frankly, there's nothing wrong with me either."

I kiss him goodbye on the cheek and turn towards the door. But then I see Audrey follow him inside.

He follows Audrey into the club, his hand on her shoulder, wearing a military uniform that she must have given to him.

"I'm sorry," I walk over to him.

"He doesn't want to talk to you," Audrey says to me.

"I'm blind, not deaf, and I can speak for myself," he says and lowers his hand holding her shoulder. Then he turns to me. "You hurt me."

"I'm sorry."

"You hurt me the most by pitying me."

"I didn't pity you, I cared about you." I want to tell him that I have so many feelings for him.

"You did pity me, so you lied to me. You thought you were allowed to lie because I'm weak and vulnerable." He stands and looks in my direction, and I touch his arm, wishing he knew I was listening to him.

"Yes, I was injured," he removes my arm from his, "but the last thing I needed was pity. I got it from everyone else." He points with his head in Audrey's direction. But I don't think she notices; even though she's holding his hand, her eyes are looking around. Maybe she's looking for Henry.

"I didn't mean to hurt you."

"I needed someone to believe that I was strong enough to recover. You know how it is, you were there once. Of all people, you're the one who should have known pity would hurt me the most. Because that means you didn't believe in me."

"You were the wounded soldier lying in bed next to me, and I tried to take care of you. I didn't think of it as pitying you or lying to you.

I just wanted you to have enough strength to recover, isn't that enough?" I say to him.

I want to tell him that I think about him all the time and miss our conversations, but I can't say that next to Audrey. She's staring at us, holding his arm trying to move him towards the club.

"It's too late, Grace. You can't take back lies and pity."

"You're right," I say to him and step out of the club, walking towards the jeep. I wish he would have called me Gracie, then I could still believe there was a chance for forgiveness.

***

"What are you doing here at this hour?" I ask her as she exits the hospital and sits down next to me on the white stairs. I couldn't go to sleep after I came back from the club, and I was sitting alone, looking at the stars, and trying not to shiver in the cool air.

"Americana, I want to make sure I'm not like that woman in the alley in Rome." She puts her arm on my shoulder, and I offer her a cigarette, but she refuses. I was going to light one for myself, but I change my mind and put it back in the box. I need to stop with all this smoking.

"Would you let me meet your son?" I ask her after a few minutes.

"He's asleep now, Americana. You should go to bed too." She gets up from the stairs and starts walking down the dark parking lot towards her motorcycle. I can hear the sound of her footsteps on the gravel.

"Good night, la vedova en moto."

"Americana," She suddenly turns to me. "Come meet my son."

"Wait one minute." I go up to my room and get a coat. I rush back to the parking lot and sit behind her on the motorcycle hugging her tightly.

"One look and that's it, Americana, don't disturb his sleep. He dreams of angels," she says as she starts the motorcycle, slowly exiting the parking lot towards the dark road leading to the village.

We reach an alley in the village, and she stops and gets off the motorcycle. I follow her, walking slowly on the cobblestones, careful not to slip.

"Shhh... Americana," she whispers to me as she stops in front of a wooden door, opening it quietly.

Inside the house, she whispers to an older woman, and all I can understand is the words bambino and Americana as she looks at me and smiles before disappearing into the corridor, she then returns after a moment holding a three-year-old boy in her arms. He hugs her and rubs his eyes, looking at me suspiciously before putting his head on her shoulder.

"Tea?" the older woman asks me. Perhaps she is Francesca's mother, or someone who takes care of her child while she's away.

"Americana, why are you crying?" Francesca asks me after a moment.

"It's nothing," I wipe my tears. "If I ever have a child, I wish he'll be exactly like yours."

"Thank you, Americana," she says to me on our drive back to the hospital.

"Good night, la vedova en moto," I say to myself as I stand on the hospital stairs and watch her drive away back to the village and her son.

***

"Allen."

A few days after Thanksgiving, I hear a nurse walking in the hall, reading names off the list she's holding in her hand. I knew this day would come soon.

"Going home." Allen gets up from his bed and starts packing.

"Garrett."

"Going home."

I watch him shake his friends' hands, and I lower my eyes back to my book. This isn't about me anymore.

"Jeffery."

"Friends, I'm going home. We'll meet again on the other side of the Atlantic."

I should concentrate on the words in my book. I'm just a nurse who sits in the nurses' station reading a book. I don't have to be worried about the ship going back home. I got what I wanted.

"John."

"Goodbye, friends, you've been great, even though I can't see you." I can't help myself and lift my gaze. I can see John hugging Edward, who has been reading to him after I left the hall. The book I'm reading now is much more interesting.

"Kenneth." She continues to read.

"Home awaits."

At least I know that it's over. No matter what I try, he's not willing to talk to me anymore. It's fine, I don't have any feelings for him either way.

"Lester."

"Going home."

I see Audrey approaching John's
bed, helping him pack his things.
I need to stop looking at the hall,
I have a book to read. He's not
different from any other wounded
soldier I've treated.

"Raymond," the nurse continues
to read, but I no longer follow
the names on the list. I watch
the soldiers as they begin to walk
towards the ambulances waiting for
them outside, and John leaves as
well, putting his hand on Audrey's
shoulder and following her. I get up
from the nurses' station and walk
past him, trying to be as loud as
I can with my wooden leg on the
floor. Maybe he will hear me and say
something about my limp. But he
says nothing, while Audrey smiles at
me with red painted lips. Perhaps he
didn't hear my footsteps.

I come out of the building and look at them from the stairs. One by one, they get into the white ambulances parked in the front driveway, waiting for them. I try to locate John, but I can only see Audrey walking towards me. He's already in the ambulance, it's too late now. It's been too late for days, but now I can't even wave goodbye.

"I'll always remember his kiss goodbye," Audrey pauses next to me, but I don't answer her.

I cross the parking lot and go past the white ambulances, past Francesca's motorcycle parked behind the supply trucks, reaching the stone fence I crossed when I ran away the first time. I don't need to watch him leave; he doesn't want me anymore.

One by one, the ambulances drive out of the parking lot. I grab onto the stone fence and climb over it, remembering that day I fell. This time I'm not injured, and I just need to be careful not to slip. I rush and walk through the trees and manage to see the white vehicles moving away towards Naples. I suppose I can still get to the road and try to stop them, but there's no point. He's made his choice, and I tried to apologize and failed.

I watch as the ambulances become white dots in the horizon, like a flock of white birds flying to the hot south in the winter. I have to return, there's no point in standing here and looking at the empty road.

"Did he leave, Americana?" She sits in our corner and hugs me as I sit down next to her and rest my head on her shoulder. I'm not going to cry, I've cried enough in the last few months.

"Now that John is gone, you can try to be my friend again," I hear a voice and see Audrey standing near us. She holds a box of cigarettes in her hand, about to light one for herself.

"No," I say to her, "I'll never be your friend again. You'll never be able to understand Francesca and I. This friendship corner doesn't belong to you, this corner belongs to us flawed and strange women."

Audrey tries to think of an answer while lighting her cigarette, but Francesca turns to her and starts yelling at her in Italian, and Audrey backs away and leaves.

"Go find yourself a pilot," I shout after her, "but not Henry, he's too good of a man for a woman like you."

She pauses for a moment, perhaps thinking about turning around and answering me, but Francesca curses at her, and she walks away, leaving us alone.

"Americana, today it is a pleasant sunny day," Francesca says after a few minutes.

"Yes, la vedova en moto, it is a pleasant, sunny day, " I answer and hug her.

***

The newspaper headlines say that the army has broken through the German defense line in the north and is advancing towards Bologna. For several days now, transport trucks have been arriving at the mansion and the soldiers have kept loading them with all the non-essential equipment we had at the hospital.

"Grace, come into my office when you're done." Blanche walks past the operating room and pauses for a moment before disappearing in the hallway.

"Yes, Head Nurse Blanche," I mumble through the medical mask I'm wearing. What have I done now?

"Artery surgical forceps," the doctor says quietly, "did you make a fuss again?" He looks at me for a moment, but I don't answer him. Since John's departure, I've only been focused on work, trying to forget him, even though I know no one has forgotten what I've done to him.

At night I keep reading the letters Georgia wrote to him, imagining that I was the one who wrote them. I managed to grab the letters from the floor that night, but I need to forget him. We're at war, people keep coming and going, we're all war wanderers just like Henry told me.

"Grace," the surgeon says to me, "I'm done. Finish dressing him, then go, the intimidating Blanche is waiting for you."

"Yes," I smile at him as I open a new bandage and begin to dress the wound.

"So what should I do with you now, Grace?" She looks at me seated behind her desk.

"What do you mean, Head Nurse Blanche?" I stand and look at her.

"We're leaving. In a few days, the hospital is moving north. What do you want to do?

"I want to keep working with you, Head Nurse Blanche." I look at her. I don't care what people think of my wooden leg anymore.

"You know Grace, someday you'll have to return home, the war will end one day."

"There will always be another war, won't there? You're still here in this hospital."

"Yes, there will always be another

war, and I'm still here." She looks up at me and goes to her metal locker, taking out the whiskey and two glasses. "But don't be like me." She pours both of us a drink and hands me a glass.

"When did you become an army nurse?"

She remains silent for a moment as if thinking whether to answer me. "In the previous Great War," she smiles to herself and sips her whiskey. "I was very much like you back then, twenty-two or twenty-three, so excited to sail overseas and save lives. In the spring of 1917, I came to France with the wave of American soldiers."

"And why did you stay for so long?" I sip my whiskey.

"Even though I wasn't injured, after what I saw in the war I couldn't return home. I felt that whoever didn't fight wouldn't be able to understand me." She also sips her glass of whiskey. "So I stayed, because there's always another war, and I went to the Philippines, and I went to Spain to fight Franco's fascists, and now I'm here to fight the Nazis. I think I just got used to this way of life," she smiles at me and pours more whiskey into our glasses.

"You've saved a lot of lives." I look at her. There is a lot of grace in her gray hair.

"Yes, I've stopped counting by now," she hands me the glass. "But I don't want you to be like me. It's good to go home. In the end, peace will come." She raises her glass and we both take a sip.

"Anyway," she says, "if you'd like to continue with us, I'd be very happy to have you."

"I just need a jeep for half the day." I place the empty glass on the table.

"Why are you suddenly asking for permission?" She looks at me. "Get out of my office. I don't want to know about this."

"Yes, Head Nurse Blanche." I get out of her office and hurry to the parking lot, get into one of the jeeps, and pray quietly.

I hope that there is enough gas, and I hope I'll find what I'm looking for.

* * *

The pleasant afternoon sun is blinding me as I slowly cross the village on my way from Rome. Suddenly I change my mind and turn around, slowly driving back to the village.

"Geppetto, Pinocchio," the children playing on the tank call out to me and wave their hands as I stop beside them.

"Francesca," I raise my voice over the jeep's engine noise, and they jump off the tank turret and surround me.

"Francesca," I say to them as I pull a bar of chocolate out of my bag, breaking it into cubes. The tallest one, holds my hand tightly, while the boy with the wild hair laughs and chews on the chocolate cubes, and the girl quickly snatches the

cube from my hand but comes
back for more, smiling at me with a
mouth full of chocolate.

"Francesca," I say to them again,
but they don't seem to understand
me.

"La vedova en moto," I finally say,
and they yell "Si, Si" until one of
them jumps into the jeep and points
at me with his hand. Everyone else
joins him and climbs inside, and
I drive through the village streets
in a jeep full of children, laughing
and pointing me in the direction of
Francesca's house.

"Grazie," I wave to them as I park
the jeep. They wave back and run
away through the narrow street,
their mouths filled with more of
the chocolate they found in my
bag. I hold the package wrapped

in brown paper and walk carefully on the cobblestones, searching for the wooden door. Finally I see a red motorcycle parked outside and I know she's home.

"Americana, this brings bad luck," she tells me after a few minutes.

"It's not bad luck. It's a gift."

"Americana, it's bad luck when a woman buys another woman a dress."

"It's not bad luck. Sometimes bad things happen to us without a reason at all."

"It's a lot of money, you stupid Americana." Her fingers caress the soft fabric.

"La vedova en moto, I bought it on the black market."

"Did you give the money to the girl in the alley? Like I taught you?"

"Yes."

"I don't believe you."

I wipe away a tear, not telling her about the meat and milk cans. I carried the duffel bag with me and gave to her. At first she ran away from me, like a suspicious cat. She hid at an entrance to a building as I approached, and I placed the food cans on the floor and walked away, looking at her. She came out from the shadows, collected the food cans, and disappeared again. I hope Blanche won't hear about the missing cans.

"Wait here, Americana," she tells me and leaves the house. I'm left alone, sitting and smiling awkwardly at a toddler peeking from one of the rooms.

"Americana, the shoemaker almost cried when he saw them," she walks in and hands me the boots that Audrey had ruined, "but he managed to sew them up. I took them without asking you."

"Thank you, la vedova en moto." I hug her, "Thanks for everything. Even though I can get along fine without them. Walking on a wooden leg; that's who I am."

"Americana, this is for the day when you meet a nice Americano like John and want to dress up like an Italian."

"I'm an Americana, have you forgotten?"

"Good thing you're going. I won't need to clean up after you."

"I'll come visit, you're my only friend."

"Go already. I knew that in the end, you would go and leave me alone." She wipes away her tears.

"I'll think of you all the time." I have tears too.

"You're a liar. You'll forget me as soon as you drive away." She hugs me and then removes the cross from her neck, "Take it, Americana, It will protect you."

"I can't take it. It is yours."

"Americana," she puts it on my neck, "it didn't do me any good, but I'm sure it will take care of you."

"Thank you, la vedova en moto," I whisper and feel the little cross with my fingers. It hangs on a delicate necklace around my neck. I so want to believe she's right.

"Go already, Americana. It brings bad luck to cry so much." She hugs me in the alley for a long time before I get into the jeep that awaited me.

17. Chicago, Sep. 1945.

"I see you recently returned from Europe." She sits behind her dark wooden desk and peruses my discharge papers spread out on the table, while I stand tall in front of her.

"You can sit, you're no longer in the army." She points to the wooden chair in front of the desk, and I sit down. Her nurse's cap is tightly fastened to her black and silver-striped hair, and she is wearing black-framed glasses.

"I see you were here as an intern before you went to Europe, and now you want to come back since the war is over," she continues to read from the pages.

"Yes..." I want to continue the sentence and correct myself, "Yes, Head Nurse Marie."

"I also see that you were injured."

"Yes, Head Nurse Marie, but I also recovered and continued to work as a nurse, taking care of the wounded."

"There is no full recovery from such an injury." She speaks to herself while reading the papers. "This is a civilian hospital. I'm not sure how patients will react to such a nurse."

"Head Nurse Marie, I'll deal with it. In the end, people will get used to my leg. It's who I am."

She keeps on looking at the papers for some time. Then she gets up from her desk and goes to the big wooden cupboard on the side of the room, checks one of the drawers, and returns, putting two letters on the table. "They arrived some time ago, no one knew what to do with them, I kept them with your old personal documents. I don't know how they knew you would come back here."

"Thank you, Head Nurse Marie." I hold the letters and my fingers gently tear the first envelope, even though I'm sitting in front of her and it's not polite. She's just looking at my papers and not at me. She won't hire me anyway.

The first envelope is empty and contains no letter, just one picture of a woman with long, scattered black hair wearing a flowery dress, standing next to her motorcycle.

"Grace, is everything okay?" she asks me. "Bad news?"

"No, Head Nurse Marie, great news,"
I answer as I wipe away a tear
and my fingers open the second
envelope. I couldn't learn not to cry.

Dear Gracie, my eyes go over the
words.

I said a lot of bad things to you
that day when I found out what
happened, and I can only tell you
that I'm sorry for each and every
one of them.

I wanted to write to you on the
ship home to New York Harbor, but
it took me a while to gather the
courage to admit I was so wrong.
And then, wanting to apologize,
I forgot the name of the hospital
where you worked in Chicago before
the war, even though you shouted
it loudly back then when we were
standing on the road.

Twenty-seven such letters have been written by good people who helped me, to twenty-seven hospitals in Chicago. Maybe one of them will find its way to your hands and heart. But that's not what I wanted to write to you.

You didn't hurt me. You were my lifeline in the darkest times, my shield from further pain, covering my wounded body with your whispering words at night. Only my pride prevented me from admitting that I needed you more than you needed me, not because I was blind, but because your company was so pleasing to my injured soul. Grace, the touch of your fingers stirred my imagination, even though I've never seen the color of your eyes or your hair, I didn't need to, you were always beside me. You were the one I thought about every night, waiting for your words, and you were the one I fell asleep with every night in my imagination. But in the end, of all people, you were the one I wasn't willing to forgive, even though the one who had to apologize was me.

I went home to Cold Spring, but after a while I realized that the small and familiar place was too suffocating for me, surrounded by Georgia and Gerard-something. Finally I left the comforts of home for the big city of New York, even though it's more complicated there. I no longer wanted to be pre-war John, I wanted to be a John who danced with you on the ruined road, holding your waist and feeling your body close to mine.

I am learning to be blind, and I've started teaching children in a school

for the blind. Who knows, maybe I'll
also be able to go back and teach in
a regular primary school here in the
big city one day.

I don't know where the war took
you. I think you told me then
that we are all war wanderers,
and you were probably right, and
our paths have parted. Still, at
the end of every day, when I'm
on my way home, I enter Grand
Central Station, and before I get
off the train platform I stand for a
few minutes near the clock in the
center of the hall, the one above the
information post.

The woman at the counter, the one
who knows the answer to every
question in the world, didn't know
where I could find a woman with
a pleasant touch, smooth skin,
and soft lips, who wears military

uniforms and whispers to me at night. And I was ashamed to tell her that this woman saved me with her words and the touch of her fingers, and that I lost her with bad words.

So every day in the evening, on my way to the train, I stand for a few minutes under the clock and listen to the footsteps of all the people who cross the hall, trying to imagine that I can hear the sound of your funny walk.

I don't know where this war took you, but I so hope that wherever you are, you've found your love.

Sorry for hurting you,

John.

"Grace, are you sure everything's fine?" Head Nurse Marie asks me. "You're crying."

"Everything's fine," I answer her and get up from my chair, not bothering to wipe away the tears.

"Grace, where are you going?"

"Sorry," I reply to her, "but I have a train to catch."

The End

To my daughter, who asked for two more pages:

18. Grand Central Station, New York.

"Train 1503 to Philadelphia will leave platform five in three minutes," I hear the speaker announce in its metallic voice as I get off the train from Chicago.

"Train 2210 from Atlanta arriving at platform seven in two minutes," it says as I walk along with the crowd towards the stairs to the departures hall, holding my cane in my hand. I don't care if they're looking at me.

"Train 3148 to Pittsburgh will leave

platform four in two minutes," I can still hear the announcer as I climb the stairs and enter the golden hall, looking up at the high ceiling and stopping for a moment. The painted stars look down from above on all the people walking around me on their way home at the end of the day. None of them stops and stares at the cane I hold in my hand. Here I'm just one woman standing in the crowd. How will I find him?

The golden clock above the information booth in the center of the hall shows five and seventeen minutes, and I want it to tell me whether I'm early or late, and maybe this letter sent months ago is no longer meant to be.

I already know most of the words he wrote to me by heart. I haven't stopped reading the letter throughout the trip, since yesterday when I arrived at the Chicago train station and hurried to buy a ticket for the first train to New York, not stopping for a moment to think that maybe I should take a bag of clothes or at least toiletries for the long journey. Line by line I read the words as the train passed through forests and villages. Even when the sun went down and the night outside replaced the green fields, I continued reading by the light of the little lamp above my head, until the woman sitting on the bench in front of me remarked that the light was interfering with her sleep. I took out the lighter I'd kept in my bag since Italy, even though I no longer smoke, and kept reading his words.

What will I do if he doesn't come? Who keeps waiting every day for months in the same place, for a letter he sent without knowing where?

"Excuse me, Miss," a handsome Navy soldier turns to me, "how do I get from here to Times Square?"

"Sorry, I'm new here," I answer him, feeling weird to be out of uniform, and he smiles at me and hurries to ask a man in a suit who points him to the right exit.

There are still many soldiers in the crowd, rushing from and to the train platforms, but there are fewer than two years ago when I first arrived here, on my way to New York Harbor and a journey that would bring me to Italy and John. The big sign hanging on the wall, calling for the public to buy defense bonds to support the war effort, has been removed. The war is over.

I hold the letter in my hand
and slowly walk to the clock in
the center, surrounding it and
searching, but I don't see him. The
woman at the information booth
doesn't know a tall man with warm
fingers and a charming smile who
hid a chocolate bar for picnics in
his backpack and handed them to
children at the village entrance.
She politely smiles at me and turns
to the man standing in line behind
me, who asks her about the train to
Baltimore.

Could it be that I'm late? Maybe he's
no longer standing and imagining
the sound of my footsteps?

I walk to the bookstore at the side
of the hall and buy myself a travel
book, one about a heroine looking
for love and finding her man at the
end. Did he also write her a letter?

I stand at the side of the hall, flipping through the book randomly and looking at the clock in the center. Six thirty-six, how long will I wait?

"Excuse me, miss, do you want to buy a ticket?" asks the saleswoman sitting behind the barred window of the box office where I stand.

"No, thank you, I've arrived at my destination."

"So can you move aside? You're disturbing the other people in line who haven't yet arrived at their destinations."

"Sorry," I answer her and move a few steps, leaning against the white marble wall and folding dog ears in the pages. I will count to three hundred, then I'll decide.

I'll count to another three hundred, then I'll decide.

But then I see him.

He's not in uniform or the white clothes of the wounded, but brown trousers and a button-down shirt. He walks through the crowd wearing sunglasses, maybe the ones he got after breaking what I brought him. Still, he holds my wooden cane in his hand, groping his way through the people to the clock in the center of the hall, and standing next to it. In small steps he starts dancing, as he did on the ruined road, ignoring the people waiting in line for the information booth and the woman who knows everything but didn't understand that this is the man I'm looking for.

"Miss, you forgot your book," I can still hear the girl from the ticket office calling after me, but I ignore her and walk towards him, making noise with my legs and the cane I hold in my hand.

"Gracie?" He turns in my direction, his hands waiting for me.

"Yes, it's me." I hold them, feeling his warm fingers.

"I love your limp." He puts his hands on my hips and continues to dance with me. I don't care about all the people around us.

"I hate my limp, but it's part of who I am." I come close to him and bring my lips to his, touching them and kissing him.

The End

Author's Note: Pieces of History.

The Italian campaign during WW2 was a long and complex conflict full of sudden reversals, and to understand it we must go back twenty years before the outbreak of hostilities. In 1922 Benito Mussolini, called the 'Duce,' came to power in Italy and turned it into a fascist state.

His armed militias, the 'Black Shirts,' terrorized Italians who tried to oppose them, killing and wounding protestors and leaders from other parties. They are mentioned in Francesca's story of her father, who tried to go out to demonstrations and was beaten to a pulp.

Throughout his rule, the 'Duce' tried to establish Italy as an empire, and sent the Italian army to conflicts in Africa and Europe. The morale of Italian soldiers was generally low and they fought poorly, but this did not prevent Mussolini from sacrificing them for his aspirations to rule the world together with Hitler. Italian soldiers were sent to occupy Greece with no success, and later to North Africa to fight against the British and Americans. Finally, in the summer of 1941 as Germany was invading Russia, an Italian expeditionary force joined the German army; it was destroyed in the siege of Stalingrad at the end of 1942.

Francesca's husband was among those who had opposed the war and Mussolini, but were forced to enlist or be executed as traitors. He was sent to Stalingrad, where all traces of him were lost in the terrible winter of 1942.

In 1943, after the American invasion of Italy, Mussolini was deposed and the Italian government signed a surrender agreement with the Americans. But the German army continued to occupy northern Italy, stabilizing defensive lines in the mountains that prevented the Allies from advancing, and ravaging the weary Italian people. A small reminder of the suffering caused by power-hungry dictators can be found in the scene set at the ruined port of Naples, with children trying to get cigarettes to sell on the black market, the woman selling her body to survive in Rome, and the refugee convoys Grace passes on her way to Naples for the second time.

The Italian campaign fought by the Allies:

The U.S. Army began the war on Italy from afar, invading the shores of North Africa. In the fall of 1942, the soldiers of the 3rd Division (John among them) landed on the beaches north of Casablanca, in Morocco. That year, while American divisions fought in the scorching deserts of North Africa against Italian troops and Rommel's German army, the invasion of Normandy was still being planned. It would only take place a year and a half later.

The American, British, Canadian and Australian troops didn't stop in North Africa. After heavy fighting at the Battle of Kasserine Pass in Tunis, the expulsion of the German army from North Africa was completed, and in May 1943 – a year before Normandy – John and his comrades landed for the second time. This time they stormed the shores of Sicily.

In November 1943 Naples was liberated, and the retreating Germans troops began to establish defensive lines in the mountains which the Allies would have difficulty breaking through. Thus, in January 1944 the Allies landed forces from the sea for the third time, this time south of Rome in the small town of Anzio, trying to bypass the German defense lines. Once again the 3rd Division took part in the invasion from the sea. However, the German lines were not breached and the American forces remained surrounded around the small town. An attack was required to finally break through the German lines and reach the besieged American soldiers at Anzio.

At this point Grace arrives in Italy, driving north from Naples with reinforcements heading to the battlefield. Many American divisions took part in the battle for Italy. Most were National Guard divisions from the southern states; this is reflected in the names of the cities the soldiers say to Grace in the back of the truck. In addition to the American soldiers, British, Canadian, Free Polish Army, Free French Army and Jewish fighters from Israel participated in battles throughout Italy. Although all the heroes of this book are American soldiers, the many military cemeteries scattered across Italy attest to the significant contributions of the soldiers of all nations to victory in the Italian front of WW2.

The U.S. military medical force in North Africa and Italy was the 7th Medical Corps, established after Pearl Harbor and containing mostly medical personnel from Chicago, Grace's hometown. This medical force included field hospitals, ambulances and military hospitals usually housed in appropriate states after capture by the U.S. military, and converted to function as hospitals. During the war, the 7th Medical Corps treated over 30,000 wounded and saved the lives of many.

It was customary to mark ambulances and hospitals with a clear red cross, but fighting forces did not always respect this marking. Many medical personnel were injured by German planes during the fighting. I decided to open the book with a German plane attack and add another one at the hospital, making no one feel safe in this war.

The Bridges of Florence:

John, who was wounded in Florence, tells Grace that the Germans blew up all the bridges in the city to prevent the Americans from advancing. Only the oldest bridge, Ponte Vecchio – built in 1345 – was left undamaged. The bridge was not blown up because the German officer responsible for collapsing the bridge was a former student of architecture, and his heart would not let him destroy the ancient structure. Sometimes humanity and respect are revealed even in the darkest places.

Henry and the other pilots were part of the 15th Air Force, who were in charge of the Middle East and Italy theatres. They flew various types of bombers, mainly B-17s and B-24s, for bombing raids on Germany's industrial plants in northern Italy, southern Germany and fascist Romania. The percentage of casualties among the pilots and planes was high, and they showed great courage in continuing to fly again and again, bringing victory ever-closer.

Historically, the 15th Air Force's airfields were located in Foggia in southeastern Italy, a convenient landing site for constructing airfields, and close to the port of Bari from which it was easy to supply the planes with fuel and bombs. Anyone looking for these airfields today will not find them. The tin huts and wooden control towers have disappeared, replaced by agricultural fields. Only aerial photography will sometimes show the remains of the runway as a dirt road. For the sake of the story, I moved the airport close to the hospital, which was located south of Rome.

The war in Italy against the German defense lines was prolonged, and lasted until the surrender of the Nazis on May 8 1945. John's division, the 3rd Division, which began its journey in Morocco and from there moved to Italy, were again deployed to France and later on to Austria, fighting on until the end of the war.

I couldn't be exact in all the historical details. But for me, writing this book was a fascinating journey into that never-ending war on the Italian front while accompanying Grace, a nurse who struggles to recover and find love.

Thank you for reading.

Alex Amit

Made in the USA
Middletown, DE
12 August 2023

36591645R10235